CHRISTMAS STORIES

CHRISTMAS STORIES

Tales of the Season

EDITED BY JOHN MILLER

CHRONICLE BOOKS
SAN FRANCISCO

As always, thanks to K

Printed in the United States of America.
Library of Congress Cataloging in Publication Data
Christmas Stories / edited by John Miller.

p.   cm.

ISBN 0-8118-0345-7

1. Christmas—Literary collections. I. Miller, John, 1959-
PN6071.C6C56 1993
808.8'033—dc20

92-46110
CIP

Book and cover design: Big Fish Books
Composition: Jennifer Petersen, Big Fish Books
Cover Image: *The Journey of the Magi*
Sassetta (Stefano di Giovanni),
Italian (Sienese), active by 1423, d. 1450
Courtesy of The Metropolitan Museum of Art
Bequest of Maitland F. Griggs, 1943
Maitland F. Griggs Collection
© 1989 MMA

Distributed in Canada by Raincoast Books,
112 East Third Avenue, Vancouver, B. C. V5T 1C8

10 9 8 7 6 5 4 3 2 1

Chronicle Books
275 Fifth Street
San Francisco, CA 94103

TABLE OF CONTENTS

ANDREI CODRESCU

Introduction

I WAS BORN a Jew and raised a Communist, so what am I doing writing the introduction to a book of Christmas stories?

Well, the truth is that I was never a very good Communist, and I was the kind of Jew that grew up loving Christmas. I was born in the Carpathian Mountains of Romania, in an ancient German town called Sibiu, or Hermanstadt. It snowed almost as much in my town as it

---

The Romanian poet Andrei Codrescu makes his home in New Orleans, where he edits The Exquisite Corpse: A Monthly of Books and Ideas *and is a commentator for National Public Radio. Codrescu wrote his first autobiography at 23,* The Life and Times of an Involuntary Genius.

1

✳

did in a Dickens story. The Communist authorities had banned Christmas, which they had renamed "the winter holidays," but no one paid any attention to the ban. Weeks before Christmas, the old medieval houses of my burg spruced up and began sporting wreaths, decorations and twinkling lights. Walking through the paths carved in waist-high snow in the evenings, you could see Christmas trees in every window. The smell of strudels, walnut pies and roasts began wafting from behind the tall walls where German *fraus* could be heard singing as they cooked.

Miraculously, oranges appeared in the usually threadbare shops. Every day, from the first of December onward, my mother discussed with our neighbors the burning question of oranges. There were rumors as to when exactly they were supposed to arrive. I stood in line for bread and milk every morning at 6 A.M., before going to school, and listened carefully for hints about the oranges. Someone had it on good authority from the cousin of someone married to a man in the railroad administration that the oranges were due in the shops two days hence, on the 14th. A similarly authoritative source, on the other hand, claimed to have word of the oranges being sighted in a warehouse just outside of town. After many days of such agitation, the oranges finally made their brilliant, sudden, wondrous appearance in the windows of shops that were soon mobbed until the last orange vanished. The Christmas oranges, to the credit of their purveyors, were not just common oranges. They were huge, thick-skinned, individually wrapped Haifa oranges, imported from Izrael. In our bleak world, dominated by the dull greys of necessity and a general air of decay and moroseness, these bright globes of sunshine were concentrated spheres of hope. They changed our mood. We became suddenly better, kinder, sweeter. It felt almost like a sin to actually *eat* these harbingers of good news. When my mother and I finally sat down with our oranges on Christmas day, we peeled them slowly, kissed the plump slices before we actually bit them, closed our eyes and, as the heavenly juice sprayed our palate, we fancied that we were cured of everything that ailed us. (The curative powers of oranges were whispered about in awe in my home town: a single orange was said to bring a dead man to life.)

Oranges from Israel were all I knew about Christmas until my mother married a Romanian railroad engineer named Puiu, who was an Orthodox christian. I was about ten years old then, and not in the mood for a stepfather. Especially one of Puiu's generally bad temper, sour disposition and plain nastiness. I did my best to respond in kind, so my poor mother just didn't know what to do with us. We were constantly feuding. But all that changed, quite suddenly, around Christmas time. I had seen Puiu in my room (which was only a closet between the kitchen and their bedroom, but *mine*). I asked him sharply what he thought that he was doing there without a passport. He didn't answer, so I chalked up one more offense on my ever-growing list. That night I went to sleep in a very bad mood, and tossed and turned until the tenth and final version of my Nobel acceptance speech (most of which I spent excoriating the despicable Puiu) worked its magic and took me out of the world. In the middle of the night, something startled me awake. I opened my eyes and saw that my whole room was full of soft, colored snowflakes that twinkled everywhere. There were blue, red, gold, green flakes everywhere I looked. I then saw that each flake had *wings!* The soft, twinkling lights were angels. They made a soft music as they flew about the room, and I was flooded with a feeling of such joy and peace I lifted off my bed and flew between their sparkling bodies for what seemed like a long time. I then fell asleep again. When I awoke in the morning, still full in my bones with the good feeling of the tiny angels, I saw a Christmas tree at the foot of my bed. It was full of sparkling gold, orange, green, and red lights. There were soft silver globes in it, and chimes that made soft music. Under it, there were packages tied with ribbon.

Unbeknownst to me, Puiu had erected this wonder while I slept.

We had a classic Christmas that year, with Puiu's relatives from near Bucharest, some of my mother's friends, and our Hungarian next door neighbors. We ate a roasted goose, ham from a pig that Puiu's family had raised all year just for this Christmas feast, and opened presents. I unwrapped mine first. It was an orange! After dinner, everyone sang songs until their heads fell on the table and they started snoring. I stayed awake as long as I could, and when I finally went to sleep it was looking at my tree. The tiny lit angels came back and I floated with them.

One Christmas, when I was in elementary school, I went to my friend Ion's village in the high mountains. The village of Rasinari, perched on the steep Carpathian crags, looked as if it had stepped whole from an illustrated book of fairy tales. The snow was very high, but there were narrow paths leading from house to house. In the courtyard of Ion's house, dozens of members of his family, dressed in colorful holiday cottons and embroidered sheepskins, had gathered to watch the village butcher kill the Christmas pig. It should have been a gory scene, but somehow it wasn't. This pig, a fat little mountain of ham, had been carefully fattened all year for this moment. Custom called for the roasted tail, which was said to be the best part, to be awarded to the youngest child. Since Ion and I were the same age, and there was no one younger, we ended up wrestling for the delicacy. I won and, amid the general approval of Ion's tribe, I crunched down on the smoky and crisp tail. It tasted delicious. That evening, together with the village children we went caroling. We carried colorful pennants and stood before the snow-covered wooden peasant houses, singing Christmas songs. The people inside showered us with candy, plaited breads, cakes and small hand-carved wooden toys.

In Romania, Christmas was officially called "the winter holidays" until 1989. That Christmas, the Communist dictator Ceausescu was executed, and Christmas became Christmas again. I was fortunate enough to be there two days after this most memorable and historical Christmas, and I was privileged to hear the bells of churches, silent for forty years of Communism, ring again.

There is something universally moving about the Christmas of everyone's childhood, no matter how painful or how privileged the rest of that childhood was. Perhaps children resemble one another more than they resemble the adults they will eventually become. The ability to experience magic is diminished in adults. It is occasionally rekindled by the memory of an occasion, particularly Christmas. The varied stories in this book are all, in some measure, about the stubborn survival of childhood magic. One is immediately transported by the smoke-colored snow of Dylan Thomas's "A Child's Christmas in Wales." A lovely window opens onto a bittersweet past in Clarence Major's story "Ten Pecan Pies," where the battles of a lifetime come to be played—and reconciled—over some bags of pecans. It's pioneer time in America, the favorite moral ground of those who'd point to the triumph of the human spirit over material lack, and the protagonists of Laura Ingalls Wilder's "A Merry Christmas" are desperately poor, but manage to have a postcard Christmas. The Depression Christmases of Major and Wilder seem far removed from Thomas' Wales. And yet, in spite of their differences, the people in these stories all pursue the same goal: a need to share, to love, to end isolation.

James Thurber's gentle satire of the American mania for Christmas cards points to the not-so-gentle truth that this national deluge of friendliness may be concealing the guilt we feel about our busy lives, too busy to make time for family and friends. Another satire, "Christmas is a Sad Season for the Poor," by John Cheever, traces the full pathos of a Sutton Place elevator man's fall from loneliness into overconcern at Christmas time. He ends up being fired, but not before he's overstuffed and loaded down with presents he has no need for, and keeps passing down the line in a grotesque parody of the "trickle-down" economy of the Republicans.

There may be great distance in both space and time between Dostoyevski's touching account of Christmas in a Siberian labor camp and Bret Harte's epic tale of sacrifice from the days of California's gold rush, but the same human heart beats insistently in both places.

Christmas in places without snow seems incongruous, unnatural. I remember missing, after I moved to California, the bracing energy of Christmas on the East Coast, particularly in New York. The throngs of shoppers in midtown, the first snow ... these seemed as far removed from the swaying palms of Dolores Avenue in San Francisco as my childhood. In Peter Matthiessen's "The Cloud Forest," sailors aboard a ship in the tropics, end up re-creating Christmas entirely out of their sentiments, fiercely ignoring the "brilliant macaws" and the "enormous white flowers." But if snow is what one craves, there is no snow like the snow in the stories of the master of Christmas stories, Charles Dickens. Memories of Christmas places, with their people and ghosts, spring to life, making the air livelier than if a loud party had been in progress. This is a grownup's Christmas, which unlike a child's, is more full of memories than of laughter.

In the end, Christmas divides in two like Gaul: the children's Christmas, with its everpresent intensity, and the grownup's, with its inevitable sadness. Both Christmases are amply represented in this book. And there are others as well, classic ones, but I won't spoil your pleasure by recalling them all. Suffice it to say, I was glad to take on the job. I realized that I had quite a bit more Christmas in me than I had anticipated given my original circumstances.

JOHN CHEEVER

Christmas Is a Sad Season

for the Poor

HRISTMAS IS a sad season. The phrase came to Charlie an instant after the alarm clock had waked him, and named for him an amorphous depression that had troubled him all the previous evening. The sky outside his window was black. He sat up in bed and pulled the light chain that hung in front of his nose. Christmas is a very sad day of the year, he thought. Of all the millions of people in New York, I am practically the only one who has to get up in the cold

---

John Cheever is considered the best short story writer of his generation. "Christmas Is a Sad Season for the Poor" is classic Cheever: a bittersweet, yearning New York tale. The story first appeared in The New Yorker *in 1949; it is collected in* The Stories of John Cheever.

black of 6 A.M. on Christmas Day in the morning; I am practically the only one.

He dressed, and when he went downstairs from the top floor of the rooming house in which he lived, the only sounds he heard were the coarse sounds of sleep; the only lights burning were lights that had been forgotten. Charlie ate some breakfast in an all-night lunchwagon and took an elevated train uptown. From Third Avenue, he walked over to Sutton Place. The neighborhood was dark. House after house put into the shine of the street lights a wall of black windows. Millions and millions were sleeping, and this general loss of consciousness generated an impression of abandonment, as if this were the fall of the city, the end of time. He opened the iron-and-glass doors of the apartment building where he had been working for six months as an elevator operator, and went through the elegant lobby to a locker room at the back. He put on a striped vest with brass buttons, a false ascot, a pair of pants with a light-blue stripe on the seam, and a coat. The night elevator man was dozing on the little bench in the car. Charlie woke him. The night elevator man told him thickly that the day doorman had been taken sick and wouldn't be in that day. With the doorman sick, Charlie wouldn't have any relief for lunch, and a lot of people would expect him to whistle for cabs.

C HARLIE HAD been on duty a few minutes when 14 rang—a Mrs. Hewing, who, he happened to know, was kind of immoral. Mrs. Hewing hadn't been to bed yet, and she got into the elevator wearing a long dress under her fur coat. She was followed by her two funny-looking dogs. He took her down and watched her go out into the dark and take her dogs to the curb. She was outside for only a few minutes. Then she came in and he took her up to 14 again. When she got off the elevator, she said, "Merry Christmas, Charlie."

"Well, it isn't much of a holiday for me, Mrs. Hewing," he said. "I think Christmas is a very sad season of the year. It isn't that people around here ain't generous—I mean, I got plenty of tips—but, you see, I live alone in a furnished room and I don't have any family or anything, and Christmas isn't much of a holiday for me."

"I'm sorry, Charlie," Mrs. Hewing said. "I don't have any family myself. It is kind of sad when you're alone, isn't it?" She called her dogs and followed them into her apartment. He went down.

It was quiet then, and Charlie lighted a cigarette. The heating plant in the basement encompassed the building at that hour in a regular and profound vibration, and the sullen noises of arriving steam heat began to resound, first in the lobby and then to reverberate up through all the sixteen stories, but this was a mechanical awakening, and it didn't lighten his loneliness or his petulance. The black air outside the glass doors had begun to turn blue, but the blue light seemed to have no source; it appeared in the middle of the air. It was a tearful light, and as it picked out the empty street he wanted to cry. Then a cab drove up, and the Walsers got out, drunk and dressed in evening clothes, and he took them up to their penthouse. The Walsers got him to brooding about the difference between his life in a furnished room and the lives of the people overhead. It was terrible.

Then the early churchgoers began to ring, but there were only three of these that morning. A few more went off to church at eight o'clock, but the majority of the building remained unconscious, although the smell of bacon and coffee had begun to drift into the elevator shaft.

At a little after nine, a nursemaid came down with a child. Both the nursemaid and the child had a deep tan and had just returned, he knew, from Bermuda. He had never been to Bermuda. He, Charlie, was a prisoner, confined eight hours a day to a six-by-eight elevator cage, which was confined, in turn, to a sixteen-story shaft. In one building or another, he had made his living as an elevator operator for ten years. He estimated the average trip at about an eighth of a mile, and when he thought of the thousands of miles he had traveled, when he thought that he might have driven the car through the mists

❋

above the Caribbean and set it down on some coral beach in Bermuda, he held the narrowness of his travels against his passengers, as if it were not the nature of the elevator but the pressure of their lives that confined him, as if they had clipped his wings.

He was thinking about this when the DePauls, on 9, rang. They wished him a merry Christmas.

"Well, it's nice of you to think of me," he said as they descended, "but it isn't much of a holiday for me. Christmas is a sad season when you're poor. I live alone in a furnished room. I don't have any family."

"Who do you have dinner with, Charlie?" Mrs. DePaul asked.

"I don't have any Christmas dinner," Charlie said. "I just get a sandwich."

"Oh, Charlie!" Mrs. DePaul was a stout woman with an impulsive heart, and Charlie's plaint struck at her holiday mood as if she had been caught in a cloud-burst. "I do wish we could share our Christmas dinner with you, you know," she said. "I come from Vermont, you know, and when I was a child, you know, we always used to have a great many people at our table. The mailman, you know, and the schoolteacher, and just anybody who didn't have any family of their own, you know, and I wish we could share our dinner with you the way we used to, you know, and I don't see any reason why we can't. We can't have you at the table, you know, because you couldn't leave the elevator—could you?—but just as soon as Mr. DePaul has carved the goose, I'll give you a ring, and I'll arrange a tray for you, you know, and I want you to come up and at least share our Christmas dinner."

Charlie thanked them, and their generosity surprised him, but he wondered if, with the arrival of friends and relatives, they wouldn't forget their offer.

Then old Mrs. Gadshill rang, and when she wished him a merry Christmas, he hung his head.

"It isn't much of a holiday for me, Mrs. Gadshill," he said. "Christmas is a sad season if you're poor. You see, I don't have any family. I live alone in a furnished room."

"I don't have any family either, Charlie," Mrs. Gadshill said. She spoke with a pointed lack of petulance, but her grace was forced. "That is, I don't have any children with me today. I have three children and seven grandchildren, but none of them can see their way to coming East for Christmas with me. Of course, I understand their problems. I know that it's difficult to travel with children during the holidays, although I always seemed to manage it when I was their age, but people feel differently, and we mustn't condemn them for the things we can't understand. But I know how you feel, Charlie. I haven't any family either. I'm just as lonely as you."

Mrs. Gadshill's speech didn't move him. Maybe she was lonely, but she had a ten-room apartment and three servants and bucks and bucks and diamonds and diamonds, and there were plenty of poor kids in the slums who would be happy at a chance at the food her cook threw away. Then he thought about poor kids. He sat down on a chair in the lobby and thought about them.

They got the worst of it. Beginning in the fall, there was all this excitement about Christmas and how it was a day for them. After Thanksgiving, they couldn't miss it. It was fixed so they couldn't miss it. The wreaths and decorations everywhere, and bells ringing, and trees in the park, and Santa Clauses on every corner, and pictures in the magazines and newspapers and on every wall and window in the city told them that if they were good, they would get what they wanted. Even if they couldn't read, they couldn't miss it. They couldn't miss it even if they were blind. It got into the air the poor kids inhaled. Every time they took a walk, they'd see all the expensive toys in the store windows, and they'd write letters to Santa Claus, and their mothers and fathers would promise to mail them, and after the kids had gone to sleep, they'd burn the letters in the stove. And when it came Christmas morning, how could you explain it, how could you tell them that Santa Claus only visited the rich, that he didn't know about the good? How could you face them when all you had to give them was a balloon or a lollipop?

On the way home from work a few nights earlier, Charlie had seen a woman and a little girl going down

*

Fifty-ninth Street. The little girl was crying. He guessed
she was crying, he knew she was crying, because she'd
seen all the things in the toy-store windows and couldn't
understand why none of them were for her. Her mother
did housework, he guessed, or maybe was a waitress, and
he saw them going back to a room like his, with green
walls and no heat, on Christmas Eve, to eat a can of soup.
And he saw the little girl hang up her ragged stocking
and fall asleep, and he saw the mother looking through
her purse for something to put into the stocking—This
reverie was interrupted by a bell on 11. He went up, and
Mr. and Mrs. Fuller were waiting. When they wished
him a merry Christmas, he said, "Well, it isn't much of a
holiday for me, Mrs. Fuller. Christmas is a sad season
when you're poor."

"Do you have any children, Charlie?" Mrs.
Fuller asked.

"Four living," he said. "Two in the grave." The
majesty of his lies overwhelmed him. "Mrs. Leary's a crip-
ple," he added.

"How sad, Charlie," Mrs. Fuller said. She started
out of the elevator when it reached the lobby, and then
she turned. "I want to give your children some presents,
Charlie," she said. "Mr. Fuller and I are going to pay a call
now, but when we come back, I want to give you some
things for your children."

He thanked her. Then the bell rang on 4, and he

went up to get the Westons.

"It isn't much of a Christmas for me," he told them when they wished him a merry Christmas. "Christmas is a sad season when you're poor. You see, I live alone in a furnished room."

"Poor Charlie," Mrs. Weston said. "I know just how you feel. During the war, when Mr. Weston was away, I was all alone at Christmas. I didn't have any Christmas dinner or a tree or anything. I just scrambled myself some eggs and sat there and cried." Mr. Weston, who had gone into the lobby, called impatiently to his wife. "I know just how you feel, Charlie," Mrs. Weston said.

BY NOON the climate in the elevator shaft had changed from bacon and coffee to poultry and game, and the house, like an enormous and complex homestead, was absorbed in the preparations for a domestic feast. The children and their nursemaids had all returned from the Park. Grandmothers and aunts were arriving in limousines. Most of the people who came through the lobby were carrying packages wrapped in colored paper, and were wearing their best furs and new clothes. Charlie continued to complain to most of the tenants when they wished him a merry Christmas, changing his story from the lonely bachelor to the poor father and back again, as his mood changed, but this outpouring of melancholy, and the sympathy it aroused, didn't make him feel any better.

At half past one, 9 rang, and when he went up, Mr. DePaul was standing in the door of their apartment holding a cocktail shaker and a glass. "Here's a little Christmas cheer, Charlie," he said, and he poured Charlie a drink. Then a maid appeared with a tray of covered dishes, and Mrs. DePaul came out of the living room. "Merry Christmas, Charlie," she said. "I had Mr. DePaul carve the goose early, so that you could have some, you know. I didn't want to put the dessert on the tray, because I was afraid it would melt, you know, so when we have our dessert, we'll call you."

"And what is Christmas without presents?" Mr. DePaul said, and he brought a large, flat box from the hall and laid it on top of the covered dishes.

"You people make it seem like a real Christmas to me," Charlie said. Tears started into his eyes. "Thank you, thank you."

"Merry Christmas! Merry Christmas!" they called, and they watched him carry his dinner and his present into the elevator. He took the tray and the box into the locker room when he got down. On the tray, there was a soup, some kind of creamed fish, and a serving of goose. The bell rang again, but before he answered it, he tore open the DePauls' box and saw that it held a dressing gown. Their generosity and their cocktail had

begun to work on his brain, and he went jubilantly up to
12. Mrs. Gadshill's maid was standing in the door with a
tray, and Mrs. Gadshill stood behind her. "Merry
Christmas, Charlie!" she said. He thanked her, and tears
came into his eyes again. On the way down, he drank off
the glass of sherry on Mrs. Gadshill's tray. Mrs. Gadshill's
contribution was a mixed grill. He ate the lamb chop with
his fingers. The bell was ringing again, and he wiped his
face with a paper towel and went up to 11. "Merry
Christmas, Charlie," Mrs. Fuller said, and she was standing in the door with her arms full of packages wrapped
in silver paper, just like a picture in an advertisement,
and Mr. Fuller was beside her with an arm around her,
and they both looked as if they were going to cry. "Here
are some things I want you to take home to your children," Mrs. Fuller said. "And here's something for Mrs.
Leary and here's something for you. And if you want to
take these things out to the elevator, we'll have dinner
ready for you in a minute." He carried the things into the
elevator and came back for the tray. "Merry Christmas,
Charlie!" both of the Fullers called after him as he closed
the door. He took their dinner and their presents into the
locker room and tore open the box that was marked for
him. There was an alligator wallet in it, with Mr. Fuller's
initials in the corner. Their dinner was also goose, and he
ate a piece of the meat with his fingers and was washing
it down with a cocktail when the bell rang. He went up

again. This time it was the Westons. "Merry Christmas, Charlie!" they said, and they gave him a cup of eggnog, a turkey dinner, and a present. Their gift was also a dressing gown. Then 7 rang, and when he went up, Mrs. Hewing was standing in the hall, in a kind of negligee, holding a pair of riding boots in one hand and some neckties in the other. She had been crying and drinking. "Merry Christmas, Charlie," she said tenderly. "I wanted to give you something, and I've been thinking about you all morning, and I've been all over the apartment, and these are the only things I could find that a man might want. These are the only things that Mr. Brewer left. I don't suppose you'd have any use for the riding boots, but wouldn't you like the neckties?" Charlie took the neckties and thanked her and hurried back to the car, for the elevator bell had rung three times.

B Y THREE o'clock, Charlie had fourteen dinners spread on the table and the floor of the locker room, and the bell kept ringing. Just as he started to eat one, he would have to go up and get another, and he was in the middle of the Parsons' roast beef when he had to go up and get the DePauls' dessert. He kept the door of the locker room closed, for he sensed that the quality of charity is exclusive and that his friends would have been disappointed to find that they were not the only ones to try to lessen his loneliness. There were goose, turkey, chicken, pheasant, grouse, and pigeon. There were trout and salmon, creamed scallops and oysters, lobster, crab meat, whitebait, and clams. There were plum puddings, mince pies, mousses, puddles of melted ice cream, layer cakes, *Torten*, éclairs, and two slices of Bavarian cream. He had dressing gowns, neckties, cuff links, socks, and handkerchiefs, and one of the tenants had asked for his neck size and then given him three green shirts. There were a glass teapot filled, the label said, with jasmine honey, four bottles of after-shave lotion, some alabaster bookends, and a dozen steak knives. The avalanche of charity he had precipitated filled the locker room and made him hesitant, now and then, as if he had touched some wellspring in the female heart that would bury him alive in food and dressing gowns. He had made almost no headway on the food, for all the servings were preternaturally large, as if loneliness had been counted on to generate in him a brutish appetite. Nor had he opened any of the presents that had been given to him for his imaginary children, but he had drunk everything they sent down and around him were the dregs of Martinis, Manhattans, Old-Fashioneds, champagne-and-raspberry shrub cocktails, eggnogs, Bronxes and Side Cars.

His face was blazing. He loved the world, and the world loved him. When he thought back over his life, it appeared to him in a rich and wonderful light, full of astonishing experiences and unusual friends. He thought that his job as an elevator operator—cruising up and down through hundreds of feet of perilous space—demanded the nerve and the intellect of a birdman. All the constraints of his life—the green walls of his room and the months of unemployment—dissolved. No one was ringing, but he got into the elevator and shot it at full speed up to the penthouse and down again, up and down, to test his wonderful mastery of space.

A bell rang on 12 while he was cruising, and he stopped in his flight long enough to pick up Mrs. Gadshill. As the car started to fall, he took his hands off the controls in a paroxysm of joy and shouted, "Strap on your safety belt, Mrs. Gadshill! We're going to make a loop-the-loop!" Mrs. Gadshill shrieked. Then, for some reason, she sat down on the floor of the elevator. Why was her face so pale, he wondered; why was she sitting on the floor? She shrieked again. He grounded the car gently, and cleverly, he thought, and opened the door. "I'm sorry if I scared you, Mrs. Gadshill," he said meekly. "I was only fooling." She shrieked again. Then she ran out into the lobby, screaming for the superintendent.

The superintendent fired Charlie and took over the elevator himself. The news that he was out of work stung Charlie for a minute. It was his first contact with human meanness that day. He sat down in the locker room and gnawed on a drumstick. His drinks were beginning to let him down, and while it had not reached him yet, he felt a miserable soberness in the offing. The excess of food and presents around him began to make him feel guilty and unworthy. He regretted bitterly the lie he had told about his children. He was a single man with simple needs. He had abused the goodness of the people upstairs. He was unworthy.

Then up through this drunken train of thought surged the sharp figure of his landlady and her three skinny children. He thought of them sitting in their basement room. The cheer of Christmas had passed them by. This image got him to his feet. The realization that he was in a position to give, that he could bring happiness easily to someone else, sobered him. He took a big burlap sack, which was used for collecting waste, and began to stuff it, first with his presents and then with the presents for his imaginary children. He worked with the haste of a man whose train is approaching the station, for he could hardly wait to see those long faces light up when he came in the door. He changed his clothes, and, fired by a wonderful and unfamiliar sense of power, he slung his bag over his shoulder like a regular Santa Claus, went out the back way, and took a taxi to the Lower East Side.

The landlady and her children had just finished off a turkey, which had been sent to them by the local Democratic Club, and they were stuffed and uncomfortable when Charlie began pounding on the door shouting

✳

"Merry Christmas!" He dragged the bag in after him and dumped the presents for the children onto the floor. There were dolls and musical toys, blocks, sewing kits, an Indian suit, and a loom, and it appeared to him that, as he had hoped, his arrival in the basement dispelled its gloom. When half the presents had been opened, he gave the landlady a bathrobe and went upstairs to look over the things he had been given for himself.

N OW, THE landlady's children had already received so many presents by the time Charlie arrived that they were confused with receiving, and it was only the landlady's intuitive grasp of the nature of charity that made her allow the children to open some of the presents while Charlie was still in the room, but as soon as he had gone, she stood between the children and the presents that were still unopened. "Now, you kids have had enough already," she said. "You kids have got your share. Just look at the things you got there. Why, you ain't even played with the half of them. Mary Anne, you ain't even looked at that doll the Fire Department gave you. Now, a nice thing to do would be to take all this stuff that's left over to those poor people on Hudson Street—them Deckkers. They ain't got nothing." A beatific light came into her face when she realized that she could give, that she could bring cheer, that she could put a healing finger on a case needier than

※

hers, and—like Mrs. DePaul and Mrs. Weston, like Charlie himself and like Mrs. Deckker, when Mrs. Deckker was to think, subsequently, of the poor Shannons—first love, then charity, and then a sense of power drove her. "Now, you kids help me get all this stuff together. Hurry, hurry, hurry," she said, for it was dark then, and she knew that we are bound, one to another, in licentious benevolence for only a single day, and that day was nearly over. She was tired, but she couldn't rest, she couldn't rest.

DYLAN THOMAS

From *A Child's Christmas in Wales*

LWAYS ON Christmas
night there was music.

An uncle played the fiddle, a cousin sang
"Cherry Ripe," and another uncle sang "Drake's
Drum."

It was very warm in the little house.

Auntie Hannah, who had got on to the parsnip
wine, sang a song about Bleeding Hearts and
Death,

Welsh writer Dylan Thomas is known for his vivid, deeply spiritual poems, such as "And death shall have no dominion," and "Do not go gentle into that good night." His story A Child's Christmas in Wales was published posthumously in 1954.

and then another in which she said her heart
was like a Bird's Nest; and then everybody
laughed again; and then I went to bed.

Looking through my bedroom window, out into
the moonlight and the unending smoke-colored
     snow,
I could see the lights in the windows
of all the other houses on our hill and hear
the music rising from them up the long, steadily
falling night. I turned the gas down, I got
into bed. I said some words to the close and
holy darkness, and then I slept.

CLARENCE MAJOR

Ten Pecan Pies

ARM DECEMBER
morning light and shadow moved evenly on Chicka-
mauga. There were a few small clouds. The hickory trees
alongside the farmhouse facing highway 69 were majestic. They moved their limbs gently in the breeze.

At another time the four children, Gal, Grew,
B. B., and Moses, had taken two heavy burlap bags full of
pecans gathered from the ground around the hickory
trees in to their grandfather, Grady Flower, and left them
near where he sat, pale and bent and paralyzed, in his

---

*Clarence Major is the author of four novels and seven books of
poetry. Major, originally from Atlanta, now teaches creative
writing at the University of California at Davis. "Ten Pecan Pies"
was written in 1971.*

✳

silver wheelchair.

Even earlier, before their grandmother, Thursday Flower, sent them to gather the smooth oval nuts, Grady had insisted on having them all brought into his room because, he said, he wanted to *see* 'em.

Nobody suspected what he really had in mind. Certainly he knew Thursday was planning to bake ten pecan pies. She'd talked about it enough, and the children walked around smacking their lips on the imaginary richness of the pies, saying *yum yum*.

At one point while the boys were shaking the pecan trees, Thursday's black, bony face poked from a window. "You get down outta that tree, Moses, 'fore you fall and break your neck! Let Grew and B. B. swing them limbs. You too little to be up there—stay on the ground and help your sister pick 'em up!"

Now Grady had had the pecans in his room, hoarding them for a long time. Wouldn't even let the kids sample one. And Thursday herself had tried to approach the burlap bags only once days ago but Grady turned her back with his hickory walking cane. Yet Thursday had not given up. She needed pecans for the pies and the pies were for Christmas presents. And Christmas was tomorrow.

Thursday knew Grady pretty well and figured he'd give in. It was just a matter of time. It was still early morning and in time, sometime today, Grady would come around to seeing things her way.

Meanwhile, the boys were going to the woods

✳

shortly to get a tree. After that, Gal would help them cut paper decorations. Thursday had already shown them how. After supper, the children would crack pecans, and she could start the pies and the opossum and the rabbits, which her son, Slick John, would come later to kill. At that time he would also help the boys erect the tree in Grady's room. Bring a little warmth and cheer to the old man. No need to always have the tree in the front. Last year Grady never even saw the tree. Refused to leave his room the whole week from Christmas to New Year's Day. Not that *that* was so unusual: there were months and years when he saw nothing beyond his own bedroom in this huge house built by his own hands. Anyway, Thursday would bake some beans. Greens and peas, which she preferred, were scarce this time of year. She'd make plenty of corn bread loaded with crackling. She'd unpack the dry figs and place them in bowls tomorrow. There would be peanuts and oranges sent by her daughters.

Thursday left the kitchen window. She went up through the large, dark, cool house, up the back hallway, through the dining room, halfway up the front hallway, and turned into Grady's musty room. Grady was sitting before the blazing fire with a blue wool blanket over his legs. The orange light from the fireplace made his white hair seem pink. His head was hanging forward. Yes, he's asleep. Beyond him were the two bags of nuts. Grady's bed was directly behind him. Crossing in front of him and the fireplace was the only way to the burlap bags.

Thursday stood there, a few inches from him, trying to weigh the moral quality of what she was tempted to do.

If she simply took the nuts she'd have to listen for days to his rage and hatred. But then she had to listen to his anger all the time anyway. He hated her plenty and she knew he would never forgive her, first, for having had a lover years ago, and second, for her good health. So why not take the pecans and make the pies and hope for the best? How would God judge her deed? Was the Devil telling her to do this? Though she was no longer a sinner, at times when she felt herself giving in to the Devil's prodding, she'd smile to herself. The Lord will forgive because it's not for myself and it is to make others happy.

She tipped past Grady. One in each hand, Thursday started dragging the bags out of their corner. They were too heavy to lift. Stepping backwards, something hard touched her rear. She stopped. Turned. Grady was holding out his walking cane to stop her. "What you think you doing, woman?"

"These are the pecans, ain't they? I'm going to bake some pies. I *told* you, Grady." She let the bags rest against each other.

"I planted them damn pecan trees over thirty years ago!" he yelled. "They're *mine!*" His eyes bulged. Spit hung from his toothless mouth.

"Yes, but my God, Grady, you can't *eat* 'em all!" From her long skinny hands she wiped pecan dust on her red-and-white checkerboard apron. She stood there looking at her broken husband and smelling the decay of his body. She tried to keep him clean but it wasn't an easy task. His white shirt had yellow stains every morning after coffee. Sometimes he'd wet his pants. Now, almost instinctively, while she spoke, she looked to see if he was dry. He was.

"My pecans," he mumbled. Sheepishly, he looked at the flames.

She sensed she was going to win him over now. "*Lord!* I don't know what to say! Grady, sometimes I think you done lost your mind. You act like you touched in the head. The way you carry on is a shame!" She stopped and reflected on what she'd said. The tone was the important element. It had been gentle and compassionate. She had to make him feel the proper amount of shame without making him angrier.

She waited a few minutes for him to respond but he said nothing. He continued to hang his head. She left the bags where they were, out of place—closer to his chair actually—and she walked away. At his doorway she turned and saw him poking, with his smooth walking cane, at the tops of the burlap bags, trying to cover the nuts. Soon now he'd have a change of heart.

In the kitchen she began washing the sweet potatoes and humming to herself. As the dirt fell away, their dark earth-red color emerged. In any mood singing was natural. Thursday's lips began to move.

O, *sinner man what you gonna do,*

O, *sinner man what you gonna do,*

O, sinner man what you gonna do,
on Judgment Day?

The wooden bucket in which she worked was situated on a bench beneath one of the four kitchen windows. Beyond this window, at the edge of the yard, Thursday could see her youngest grandchild, little Gal, with pigtails and in a blue cotton dress, feeding the fat opossum through the hole in the top of his makeshift box in which he'd been kept now for seven weeks. The box was on short stilts. There were two other wooden boxes arranged the same way, with one side of each made of screen, and with a hole in the top. In each of these was a fat rabbit. The opossum was black and gray. The rabbits were brown and white. When Gal finished feeding the opossum, she patiently stuffed carrots and corn and bread crumbs, the same stuff she'd fed the prehensile-tailed creature, into the rabbit boxes. The wild animals had been caught by the boys in traps set in the woods. And, along with her usual duty of feeding the chickens, Thursday had assigned Gal to the task of fattening these restless animals for slaughter and ultimately for the delight of the holiday season. Watching the little girl, Thursday was aware that Gal had become attached to the animals and this was bad.

Apparently Gal had already fed the chickens because Thursday could hear the hens in the yard making a fuss over the feed. And the rooster grumbling. It was midday and this was the second feeding. Slick John would not come until five or six. By then maybe Grady would give up the pecans. Thursday now remembered she had earlier sent Moses to the cellar, a damp, dark, musty place beneath the house, to get more sweet potatoes. What was he doing down there? Loafing? And B. B. was taking an awful long time to feed the hogs. By now he should be bringing in the wood Grew was chopping out near the fig tree. She could hear the ax screeching in the wood each time it struck.

Soon the boys finished their chores and went off to the woods for the tree. Grew carried on his shoulder the long two-handled saw and B. B. and Moses carried the ropes. Though it was early afternoon the ground and undergrowth and bushes were still slightly damp from the night because the sunlight this time of year was not very powerful. They went single file deep into the forest, searching for and reexamining trees they had already tentatively selected. It had to be the very best evergreen they could find. It should be straight and tall and noble. It would be a thing they'd erect in the house, and it had to have the finest qualities possible. They stopped, reconsidered, and rejected several before they found the right one—one they had not previously seen—at the edge of the canyon where the Indians used to commit suicide. When they saw it they each knew it and there was no need to say anything.

But they had to be careful. This prince of an evergreen was right on the very edge, and if it were cut down the wrong way they'd lose it in the canyon. B. B. worked at one end of the saw and Grew at the other. Moses, pulling on a rope tied by lanky Grew midway up the sturdy tree, desperately tried to direct the way it would fall; and, if he was successful, this meant he'd have to move pretty fast, since he was struggling with the rope right on the spot where the prize would fall.

The landing went well. Moses jumped to safety, and right away they started roping in the limbs to make it easier to carry.

Still, it was not easy getting it out of the woods. The path was narrow and dense and there was no road that led to their place.

When they arrived at the edge of the backyard, they saw their uncle Slick John wiping his hands on an old rag. His hands and clothes were bloody. Near him, spread out on the grass, were the slaughtered opossum and the two rabbits. Standing nearby next to the hedges was Gal, sobbing. She continued to cry with her thumb in her mouth and kept her eyes closed. The boys put down the tree to rest. They stood watching. A white hen was standing on the edge of the huge black kettle in which Thursday made lye soap. The rest of the chickens had gone away in fear of the killing and were now scur-rying around the far side of the fig tree and the grapevine on stilts at the left side of the house.

Thursday stood on the back porch with a pan of water in her hands. She too was silently watching.

Slick, a little drunk as usual, smelling of cheap moonshine, finished cleaning his hands and went over to Gal. He squatted before her. She was his favorite. He took her in his big dirty arms. "Honey, don't you know people have to eat? It doesn't mean we don't like the animals. We just have to eat. They eat. You see they kill each other to eat. And besides, tomorrow is Christmas. Don't you want to have a happy Christmas dinner?"

She did not answer, but Slick John gently rocked her little body in his arms. A bubble of snot formed at the tip of her nose. And she laughed when it popped.

Hearing her laugh, Slick said, "Thatta girl."

The boys picked up the tree and brought it up into the yard and let it down again at the steps. They did not want to watch Slick John pet Gal. He never showed them any sort of affection.

Slick went over and looked at the tree. "Pretty fine tree. Y'all getting to be experts." He smiled. "I'll help you put it up."

After the tree stood erect in Grady's room, Thursday asked Slick John to try and talk to Grady about the pecans. He said he would try.

But it didn't work. Thursday waited in the hallway. Slick John came out. "He won't give 'em up, Ma. Just be patient with him. You know Pa."

Sure, she knew Pa all right.

The evergreen smelled good in the house. Slick John left to go home to his wife, Lucy. The children sat on the floor cutting out red, blue, green, yellow, silver, gold, purple, and orange paper strips, circles, triangles, stars, diamonds, loops, and bells to decorate the tree. Its odor mingled with the cooking smells coming from the

✳

kitchen. Though they'd had supper already, the aroma of the Christmas food pervading the house made them imagine they were hungry again. The pungent smells of baked sweet potatoes, beans, and wild meat swam in torrents throughout the house and beyond. As they used their blunt scissors, they chattered away about the glory of tomorrow.

They were on the floor near the tree. Grady was in front of the fireplace. The fire was weak, it needed wood. As the children talked among themselves, Thursday stood in the doorway behind them. They were unaware of her presence until she spoke. "Tomorrow is going to be a big heartbreak if your grandpa don't give us the pecans." She said it loud enough for the old man to hear.

They looked up at her face. But she was looking at her husband there across the room.

She went over to his side and touched him.

"Grady." Her voice was low and smooth but firm. "The pecans was for the pies. It's not like I'm asking you for something for myself. You may hate me, but this is wrong. Lord knows you're wrong. I want to give our son and his wife two pies. And Mr. Hain Alcock. And Apostle Moskrey. I want to send some to our daughters too. And old folks who are alone out in Remus Road. Them people don't have nobody who care about them. They could just as well be dead. I figure the least I could do is give them a nice pecan pie on Christmas day. I was going to take them over there myself. . ."

Grady was pretending he hadn't heard. He looked at her quickly, then looked away nervously at the burlap bags. Then at the flames jumping in the fireplace.

"You know that set of books the judge gave you for Christmas when you was a little boy? Well, I was thinking about them today. They still in that closet over there, and I know they must have made you pretty happy. You kept them all these years. Took 'em with you to architecture school. They meant something to you. I know a pie ain't important as books, but a person living alone with nobody might really be thankful to get one. Just like you was about the books."

He looked again at Thursday.

The children snickered.

"Thursday," he murmured, "what you waiting for? The pecans over here in the corner." He touched the bags with his cane, quickly and lightly, a magician about to make magic. "By the time you get to 'em they'll be rotted away."

Thursday suddenly kissed the side of his face. The first time in years. The old man hardly knew how to react. He blushed. He took a deep breath and spoke. "Now, would you give me my pipe—and take these dusty bags outta my way?"

Already the children were laughing. Gal clapped her hands together and shrieked. "Grandma kissed grandpa!"

Thursday gave him his pipe and lit it for him and he smoked it with enjoyment. Grew and B. B. helped her drag the bags of nuts into the kitchen.

After Thursday helped Grady to bed, the children soon finished decorating the tree and went with her to the kitchen to crack nuts. The four of them, up past their bedtime, sat around the table using the nutcrackers—homemade gadgets. Some of the sweet oily kernels they popped into their mouths and ate. Meanwhile, Thursday worked skillfully with the eggs and butter, the vanilla and pecans she kept taking from a pile on the table. While the children cracked nuts, she beat more eggs and mixed more butter. The huge black stove continued to roar. Once in awhile Grew added a piece of wood to its fire. Thursday started humming and soon was singing.

Two big hoss's hitched to a slide,
Me and my Jesus gonna take a ride.
And the children joined her, remembering the song from church. But as they sang, they kept their voices low so as not to wake Grady.

Before long Gal fell asleep with her face on the table and pretty soon Moses could not keep his eyes open either. He kept nodding. Grew and B. B. kept breaking the smooth-shelled nuts and occasionally eating the tasty kernels.

Finally, though, even Grew and B. B. gave in to sleepiness and Thursday said, "Y'all better go to bed." It was already past midnight.

Once the boys were asleep in their room and Gal in Thursday's bed, Thursday returned to the kitchen and finished baking the pies. The children had supplied enough pecans. She worked on with the patience of a miller until the rooster crowed and daylight turned at the edges of the windows where the old green shades never fully covered them. Now, once the rooster started, he kept up his arrogant sound for over an hour.

Thursday finished the ten pies and the wild meat and the vegetables and placed them on the large table to cool. She dumped a little water on the fire in the pit of the stove. It made a sizzling sound and stopped suddenly. Yet the warmth stayed.

L AURA I NGALLS W ILDER

A Merry Christmas

EXT MORNING,
snow was in the air. Hard bits of snow were leaping and
whirling in the howling wind.

Laura could not go out to play. In the stable, Spot
and Pete and Bright stood all day long, eating the hay
and straw. In the dugout, Pa mended his boots while Ma
read to him again the story called *Millbank*. Mary sewed
and Laura played with Charlotte. She could let Carrie
hold Charlotte, but Carrie was too little to play with

---

*Laura Ingalls Wilder was one of the first women to depict life on
the American frontier. She is known for her autobiographical
Little House series of books, including the immensely popular
Little House on the Prairie. "A Merry Christmas" is from her
1937 novel* On the Banks of Plum Creek.

❋

paper dolls; she might tear one.

That afternoon, when Carrie was asleep, Ma beckoned Mary and Laura. Her face was shining with a secret. They put their heads close to hers, and she told them. They could make a button-string for Carrie's Christmas!

They climbed onto their bed and turned their backs to Carrie and spread their laps wide. Ma brought them her button-box.

The box was almost full. Ma had saved buttons since she was smaller than Laura, and she had buttons her mother had saved when her mother was a little girl. There were blue buttons and red buttons, silvery and goldy buttons, curved-in buttons with tiny raised castles and bridges and trees on them, and twinkling jet buttons, painted china buttons, striped buttons, buttons like juicy blackberries, and even one tiny dog-head button. Laura squealed when she saw it.

"Sh!" Ma shushed her. But Carrie did not wake up.

Ma gave them all those buttons to make a button-string for Carrie.

After that, Laura did not mind staying in the dugout. When she saw the outdoors, the wind was driving snowdrifts across the bare frozen land. The creek was ice and the willow tops rattled. In the dugout she and Mary had their secret.

They played gently with Carrie and gave her

everything she wanted. They cuddled her and sang to her and got her to sleep whenever they could. Then they worked on the button-string.

Mary had one end of the string and Laura had the other. They picked out the buttons they wanted and strung them on the string. They held the string out and looked at it, and took off some buttons and put on others. Sometimes they took every button off, and started again. They were going to make the most beautiful button-string in the world.

One day Ma told them that this was the day before Christmas. They must finish the button-string that day.

They could not get Carrie to sleep. She ran and shouted, climbed on benches and jumped off, and skipped and sang. She did not get tired. Mary told her to sit still like a little lady, but she wouldn't. Laura let her hold Charlotte, and she jounced Charlotte up and down and flung her against the wall.

Finally, Ma cuddled her and sang. Laura and Mary were perfectly still. Lower and lower Ma sang, and Carrie's eyes blinked till they shut. When softly Ma stopped singing, Carrie's eyes popped open and she shouted, "More, Ma! More!"

But at last she fell asleep. Then quickly, quickly, Laura and Mary finished the button-string. Ma tied the ends together for them. It was done; they could not change one button more. It was a beautiful button-string.

That evening after supper, when Carrie was sound asleep, Ma hung her clean little pair of stockings from the table edge. Laura and Mary, in their nightgowns, slid the button-string into one stocking.

Then that was all. Mary and Laura were going to bed when Pa asked them, "Aren't you girls going to hang your stockings?"

"But I thought," Laura said, "I thought Santa Claus was going to bring us horses."

"Maybe he will," said Pa. "But little girls always hang up their stockings on Christmas Eve, don't they?"

Laura did not know what to think. Neither did Mary. Ma took two clean stockings out of the clothes-box, and Pa helped hang them beside Carrie's. Laura and Mary said their prayers and went to sleep, wondering.

In the morning Laura heard the fire crackling. She opened one eye the least bit, and saw lamplight, and a bulge in her Christmas stocking.

She yelled and jumped out of bed. Mary came running, too, and Carrie woke up. In Laura's stocking, and in Mary's stocking, there were little paper packages, just alike. In the packages was candy.

Laura had six pieces, and Mary had six. They had never seen such beautiful candy. It was too beautiful to eat. Some pieces were like ribbons, bent in waves. Some were short bits of round stick candy, and on their flat ends were coloured flowers that went all the way through. Some were perfectly round and striped.

In one of Carrie's stockings were four pieces of that beautiful candy. In the other was the button-string. Carrie's eyes and her mouth were perfectly round when she saw it. Then she squealed, and grabbed it and squealed again. She sat on Pa's knee, looking at her candy and her button-string and wriggling and laughing with joy.

Then it was time for Pa to do the chores. He said, "Do you suppose there is anything for us in the stable?" And Ma said, "Dress as fast as you can, girls, and you can go to the stable and see what Pa finds."

It was winter, so they had to put on stockings and shoes. But Ma helped them button up the shoes and she pinned their shawls under their chins. They ran out into the cold.

Everything was grey, except a long red streak in the eastern sky. Its red light shone on the patches of grey-white snow. Snow was caught in the dead grass on the walls and roof of the stable and it was red. Pa stood waiting in the stable door. He laughed when he saw Laura and Mary, and he stepped outside to let them go in.

There, standing in Pete's and Bright's places, were two horses.

They were larger than Pet and Patty, and they were a soft, red-brown colour, shining like silk. Their

❅

manes and tails were black. Their eyes were bright and gentle. They put their velvety noses down to Laura and nibbled softly at her hand and breathed warm on it.

"Well, flutterbudget!" said Pa, "and Mary. How do you girls like your Christmas?"

"Very much, Pa," said Mary, but Laura could only say, "Oh, Pa!"

Pa's eyes shone deep and he asked, "Who wants to ride the Christmas horses to water?"

Laura could hardly wait while he lifted Mary up and showed her how to hold onto the mane, and told her not to be afraid. Then Pa's strong hands swung Laura up. She sat on the horse's big, gentle back and felt its aliveness carrying her.

All outdoors was glittering now with sunshine on snow and frost. Pa went ahead, leading the horses and carrying his ax to break the ice in the creek so they could drink. The horses lifted their heads and took deep breaths and whooshed the cold out of their noses. Their velvety ears pricked forward, then back and forward again.

Laura held to her horse's mane and clapped her shoes together and laughed. Pa and the horses and Mary and Laura were all happy in the gay, cold Christmas morning.

JAMES THURBER

Merry Christmas

I

T DIDN'T surprise me
to learn that Americans send out a billion and a half
Christmas cards every year. That would have been my
guess, give or take a quarter of a billion. Missing by 250
million is coming close nowayears, for what used to be
called astronomical figures have now become the figures
of earth. I am no longer staggered by the massive, but I
can still be shaken by the minor human factors involved
in magnificent statistics. A national budget of 71 thou-

James Thurber set much of the tone for the original New
Yorker *magazine, contributing scores of hilarious stories,
essays, and cartoons.* "Merry Christmas" *is from* Alarms and
Diversions, *a 1957 collection of his writings.*

sand million is comprehensible to students of our war-like species, but who is to account for the rising sales of vodka in this nation—from 108,000 bottles in 1946 to 32,500,000 bottles in 1956? The complexities of federal debt and personal drinking are beyond my grasp, but I think I understand the Christmas card situation, or crisis.

It disturbed me to estimate that two-fifths of the 1956 Christmas cards, or six hundred million, were received by people the senders barely knew and could count only as the most casual of acquaintances, and that approximately thirty million recipients were persons the senders had met only once, in a bar, on a West Indies cruise, at a doctor's office, or while fighting a grass fire in Westchester. The people I get Christmas cards from every year include a Jugoslav violist I met on the *Leviathan* in 1925, the doorman of a restaurant in Soho, a West Virginia taxi driver who is writing the biography of General Beauregard, the young woman who cured my hiccoughs at Dave Chasen's in 1939 (she twisted the little finger of my left hand and made me say Garbo back-ward), innumerable people who know what to do about my eye and were kind enough to tell me so in hotel lobbies and between the acts of plays, seven dog owners who told me at Tim's or Bleeck's that they have a dog exactly like the one I draw, and a lovely stranger in one of these saloons who snarled at a proud dog owner: "The only dog that looks like the dog this guy draws is the dog this guy draws."

The fifteen hundred million annual Yuletide greetings are the stamp and sign of the American character. We are a genial race, as neighborly abroad as at home, fond of perpetuating the chance encounter, the golden hour, the unique experience, the prewar vacation. "I think this calls for a drink" has long been one of our national slogans. Strangers take turns ordering rounds because of a shared admiration or disdain, a suddenly discovered mutual friend in Syracuse, the same college fraternity, a similar addiction to barracuda fishing. A great and lasting friendship rarely results, but the wife of each man adds the other's name to her Christmas list. The American woman who has been married ten years or longer, at least the ones I know, sends out about two hundred Christmas cards a year, many of them to persons on the almost forgotten fringe of friendship.

I had the good luck to be present one December afternoon in the living room of a couple I know just as the mail arrived. The wife asked if we minded her glancing at the cards, but she had already read one. "My God!" she exclaimed. "The Spragues are still together! They were this really charming couple we met in Jamaica eight years ago. He had been a flier, I think, and had got banged up, and then he met Marcia—I think her name was Marcia." She glanced at the card again and said, "Yes, Marcia. Well, Philip was on leave in Bermuda and he saw her riding by in a carriage and simply knew she was the girl, although he had never laid eyes on her before in his life, so he ran out into the street and jumped up on the carriage step, and said, 'I'm going to marry you! Would you believe it, he didn't even tell her his name, and of course he didn't know her from Adam—or Eve, I guess I ought to say—and they were married. They fell in love and got married in Bermuda. Her family was terribly opposed to it, of course, and so was his when they found out about hers, but they went right ahead anyway. It was the most romantic thing I ever heard of in my life. This was four or five years before we met them, and—"

"Why are you so astonished that they are still together?" I asked.

"Because their meeting was a kind of third-act curtain," said my friend's husband. "Boy meets girl, boy gets girl—as simple as that. All that's left is boy loses girl. Who the hell are Bert and Mandy?" he asked, studying a Christmas card.

Another greeting card category consists of those persons who send out photographs of their families every year. In the same mail that brought the greetings from Marcia and Philip, my friend found such a conversation piece. "My God, Lida is enormous!" she exclaimed. I don't know why women want to record each year, for two or three hundred people to see, the ravages wrought upon them, their mates, and their progeny by the artillery of time, but between five and seven per cent of Christmas cards, at a rough estimate, are family groups, and even the most charitable recipient studies them for little signs of dissolution or derangement. Nothing cheers a woman more, I am afraid, than the proof that another woman is letting herself go, or has lost control of her figure, or is clearly driving her husband crazy, or is obviously drinking more than is good for her, or still doesn't know what to wear. Middle-aged husbands in such photographs are often described as looking "young enough to be her son," but they don't always escape so easily, and a couple opening envelopes in the season of mercy and good will sometimes handle a male friend or acquaintance rather sharply. "Good Lord!" the wife will say. "Frank looks like a sex-crazed shotgun slayer, doesn't he?" "Not to me," the husband may reply. "To me he looks more like a Wilkes-Barre dentist who is being sought by the police in connection with the disappearance of a choir singer."

Anyone who undertakes a comparative analysis of a billion and a half Christmas cards is certain to lose his way once in a while, and I now find myself up against more categories than I can handle. Somewhere in that vast tonnage of cardboard, for example, are—I am just guessing now—three hundred million cards from firms, companies, corporations, corner stores, and other tradespeople. In the old days they sent out calendars for

✳

the New Year, and skipped Christmas, but I figure they are now responsible for about a fifth of the deluge. Still another category includes inns, bars, restaurants, institutions, councils, committees, leagues, and other organizations. One of my own 1956 cards came from the Art Department of Immaculate Heart College, in Los Angeles, whose point of contact with me has eluded my memory. A certain detective agency used to send me a laconic word every December, but last year, for some disturbing reason, I was struck off the agency's list. I don't know how I got on it in the first place, since I have never employed a private investigator to shadow anybody, but it may be that I was one of the shadowed. The agency's slogan is "When we follow him he stays followed," and its card was invariably addressed to "Mr. James Ferber." This hint of alias added a creepy note to the holidays, and, curiously enough, the sudden silence has had the same effect. A man who is disturbed when he hears from a detective agency, and when he doesn't, may be put down, I suppose, as a natural phenomenon of our nervous era.

I suddenly began wondering, in one of my onsets of panic, what becomes of all these cards. The lady in my house who adds two hundred items to the annual avalanche all by herself calmed my anxiety by telling me that most of them get burned. Later, I found out, to my dismay, that this is not actually true. There are at least nine

※

million little girls who consider Christmas cards too beautiful to burn, and carefully preserve them. One mother told me that her garage contains fifteen large cartons filled with old Christmas cards. This, I am glad to say, is no problem of mine, but there is a major general somewhere who may have to deal with it one of these years if the accumulation becomes a national menace, hampering the movement of troops.

Ninety per cent of women employ the annual greeting as a means of fending off a more frequent correspondence. One woman admitted to me that she holds at least a dozen friends at arm's, or year's, length by turning greeting cards into a kind of annual letter. The most a man will consent to write on a Christmas card is "Hi, boy!" or "Keep pitching," but a wife often manages several hundred words. These words, in most instances, have a way of dwindling with the march of the decades, until they become highly concentrated and even cryptic, such as "Will you ever forget that ox bice cake?" or "George says to tell Jim to look out for the 36." Thus the terrible flux of December mail is made up, in considerable part, of the forgotten and the meaningless. The money spent on all these useless cryptograms would benefit some worthy cause by at least three million dollars.

The sex behind most of the billion and a half Christmas cards is, of course, the female. I should judge that about 75,000,000 cards are received annually by

❉

women from former cooks, secretaries, and hairdressers, the formerness of some of them going back as far as 1924. It is not always easy for even the most experienced woman card sender to tell an ex-hairdresser from someone she met on a night of high wind and Bacardi at Cambridge Beaches in Bermuda. The late John McNulty once solved this for my own wife by saying, "All hairdressers are named Dolores." The wonderful McNulty's gift of inspired oversimplification, like his many other gifts, is sorely missed by hundreds of us. McNulty and I, both anti-card men, never exchanged Christmas greetings, except in person or on the phone. There was a time when I drew my own Christmas cards, but I gave it up for good after 1937. In that year I had drawn what purported to be a little girl all agape and enchanted in front of a strangely ornamented Christmas tree. The cards were printed in Paris and mailed to me, two hundred of them, in Italy. We were spending Christmas in Naples. The cards were held up at the border by the Italian authorities, agents of Mussolini who suspected everything, and returned to Paris. "I should think," commented an English friend of mine, "that two hundred copies of any drawing of yours might well give the authorities pause."

One couple, to conclude this survey on an eerie note, had sent out the same engraved Christmas card every year. Last time "From John and Joan" had under-

❉

gone a little change. Joan had crossed out "John and." Her friends wonder just how many of these cheery greetings the predeceased Joan has left. So passed one husband, with only a pencil stroke to mark his going. Peace on earth, good will to women.

August Strindberg

The Respite

A VALLEY BASIN surrounded with steep black rocks. At the back stands a large pair of scales, where newcomers are weighed.

The Deemster and his Wife sitting at a table.

The Witch comes in with a large basket.

Swedish playwright August Strindberg's early dramas were essentially biting attacks on the Christian church. These ruthless, sparse plays led to his being prosecuted for blasphemy and, eventually, to a dramatic nervous breakdown in 1899. "The Respite" is typical of his lifelong obsession with spirituality.

The Deemster. What's that?

The Witch. Christmas presents for the righteous. They
   are peep-shows. [*Gives him one.*] There you are. It
   costs nothing.

The Deemster. See, there is one kind human being at least!
   A little attention at my years and to a man of my
   standing honours your good taste and your kind
   heart.

The Witch. You are altogether too courteous, Deemster;
   but don't take it amiss if I have thought of the
   others a little, too.

The Deemster [*piqued*]. Infernal old woman, are you
   chaffing me?

The Witch [*spitting in his face*]. Shame on you! Petti-fog-
   ger!

The Deemster. Think what company one can run into!

The Witch. Isn't it good enough for you, you old perjurer,
   bribe-taker, forger, inheritance-thief, corrupter?
   Look into the peep-show and you'll see the great
   tableau, *From the Cradle to the Grave.* There
   you'll find the whole biography and all the vic-
   tims—just look! There!

[*The Deemster looks into the peep-show, and rises in fear.*]

The Witch. I hope the little remembrance will help
   toward your Christmas joy!

   [*She gives the Wife a peep-show and continues to
distribute them among the others.*]

The Deemster. What do you see?

The Wife. Everything is there; everything! And have
you noticed everything is black? The long
bright life is dark, the moments I thought innocent joy stand forth loathsome, fetid, criminal,
almost! It is as if one's memories, even the most
beautiful, had become rotten—

The Deemster. Yes, you are right; not one memory can
light up this darkness. When I see her, my
youth's first love, I see a corpse; when I bring to
mind the good Amalia there appears—a harlot;
the little children make faces at me like so many
street urchins; my house is a pigsty, the vineyard
a dump-heap with thistles; when I think of the
green forest it turns into snuff-brown leafage,
and the trunks are white as masts; the blue river
flows onward as from a barnyard, and the blue
sky above is like a smoky ceiling. Even the sun I
remember only as a name, and that which is
called the moon and shone like a lamp over
inlets and groves in the evenings of youth and
love, I remember only as—No, I can't recall them
any more. Only words remain with me, though
they are but sounds without meaning.... Love,
wine, song! Flowers, children, happiness!—Do
not the words sound beautiful? And that is all
that is left!—Love! What was love!

✳

The Wife. What was it? Two cats on the roof of a back-house.

The Deemster [*idiotically*]. That's so! And three dogs on a street corner. It's delightful to recall.

The Wife [*pressing his hand*]. It is delightful.

The Deemster [*looking at his watch*]. My watch has stopped. I am so hungry; but I am thirsty too, and I long for tobacco. But I am tired too and would like to sleep. All my habits are awake; they scratch and urge me, and I cannot gratify one of them. Unfortunate we are! Unfortunate!

The Wife. And I long for a cup of tea so much that I cannot describe it.

The Deemster. Hot green tea. That is just what I would like now; and with a little, just a little rum.

The Wife. No, not rum: I should prefer cake—

The Prince [*coming forward*]. With frosting on top? Yes, if you will sing for it.

The Wife. This rude talk tortures me more than anything else.

The Prince. That's because you don't know how what is coming will torture you.

The Deemster. What is that?

The Wife. No! Silence! We don't want to know! Silence!

The Prince. Yes! I want you to know. It begins with——

The Wife [*holding hands over ears and shouting*]. Have pity! Keep quiet, keep quiet; keep quiet!

The Prince. No, indeed, I won't keep quiet. Brother-in-law
is curious, and he shall be told. The second letter
is H.

The Deemster. This uncertainty tortures me more than
anything—Speak out, devil, or kill me!

The Prince. Kill? Ha, ha! Here we are all deathless, soul
and body, what little is left. However . . . the
third letter is—Now you'll know more!

*The Gray-Clad One enters, a small emaciated man with
gray clothes, gray face, black lips, gray beard and
hands. He speaks in an undertone.*

The Gray-Clad One. May I have a little talk with you,
lady?

The Wife [*rising frightened*]. What about?

The Gray-Clad One [*smiles maliciously*]. I will tell you . . .
out there.

The Wife [*weeping*]. No, no, I don't want to!

The Gray-Clad One [*laughing*]. It is not dangerous. Come
along! I only want to talk to you a little. Come!

[*They go out back.*]

The Prince. A little whipping for a Christmas present
does one good.

The Deemster. Do you mean to maltreat a woman?

The Prince. Here every injustice is effaced, and woman is
on a level with man.

The Deemster. Devil!

The Other [*coming forward*]. Well, how about animal

magnetism? It can work wonders with brutes.

The Deemster. I understand nothing of all this!

The Other. That is just what is intended. It is a beautiful confession from you that there are things you do not understand.

The Deemster. Assuming that I am in Hades—

The Other. Say Hell. That's what it's called.

The Deemster [stammering]. Then ... then I would point out that He who came down here once to redeem the damned——

> [*The Prince, at a wink from the Other, strikes the Deemster on the mouth.*]

The Prince. Don't reason!

The Deemster. They will not hear me! That is utter despair! Without mercy, without hope, without end!

The Other. True. Only justice and retribution exist here, justice above everything, an eye for an eye, a tooth for a tooth. Just as you wished to have it.

The Deemster. But among humankind there is pardon that does not exist here.

The Other. Only the rules can pardon. And as a jurist you ought to know that a petition for pardon must be filed in order to receive consideration.

The Deemster. For me there is no mercy!

The Other [signing to the Prince, who goes aside]. You consider your guilt too great, then?

✳

The Deemster. Yes.

The Other. Then I will speak to you with kindness. You see, there is always an end if only there is a beginning; and you have made a beginning. But the continuation is long and difficult.

The Deemster. Oh! God is good!

The Other. You have said it.

The Deemster. But ... there is one thing that cannot be undone—there is one!

The Other. You mean the Monstrance that should have been gold, but became silver? Very well. Don't you believe that He who changed water into wine can transform silver into gold?

The Deemster [*on his knees*]. But my misdeed is greater, greater than can ever be forgiven.

The Other. Now you are overrating yourself again! But rise now, for we are to celebrate Christmas in our way.—The sun never reaches us down here, as you know, nor the moon either, but tonight, tonight only, a star rises so high over the mountains that it is seen from here below. It is that star that lights the shepherd's way in the desert. It is the Morning Star.

> [*He claps his hands. The Wife comes in, quiet and peacefully happy; she goes to the Deemster and gives him her hand comfortingly. The scene is filled with shad-*

ows that all gaze up toward the mountain
at the back. Voices are heard singing,
accompanied only by violins and harps].

Voices. Puer natus est nobis;

Et Filius datus est nobis;

Cujus imperium super humerum Ejus;

Et vocabitur nomen Ejus

Magni consilii Angelus.

Chorus. Cantate Domino canticum novum,

Quia mirabilia fecit.

[Now the Star appears over the mountain.
All fall on their knees. Part of the rock is
pushed to one side.

Tableau: the Manger, with the Mother
and Child. The Shepherds are praying at
left, the three Kings at right.]

Chorus. Gloria in excelsis Deo

Et in terra pax

Hominibus bonae voluntatis!

FRANK CAPRA

It's a Wonderful Life

XT: BRIDGE AT

RAILING—NIGHT

CLOSEUP—George. He stares down at the water, desperate, trying to make up his mind to act. He leans over looking at the water, fascinated, glances furtively around him, hunches himself as though about to jump.

MED. CLOSE SHOT—From above George a body hur-

Frank Capra wrote and directed some of the most beloved films of our time, including Mr. Smith Goes to Washington, Meet John Doe, *and* It Happened One Night. *The classic Christmas staple* It's a Wonderful Life *became his best-known film because of a copyright oversight, which led to free (and innumerable) television broadcasts.*

tles past and lands in the water with a loud splash. George looks down, horrified.

Voice (from river): Help! Help!

George quickly takes off his coat, and dives over the railing into the water.

CLOSER ANGLE—George comes up, sees the man flailing about in the water, and camera pans with him as he swims toward the man.

MAN : Help! Help! Help!

EXT. TOLL HOUSE ON BRIDGE—NIGHT

CLOSE SHOT—The toll house keeper, hearing the cries for help, comes running out on the bridge with a flashlight, which he shines on the two figures struggling in the water below.

EXT. RIVER—NIGHT

CLOSE SHOT—The man in the water is Clarence, the angel whose voice we have heard speaking from Heaven. George reaches him, grabs hold of him, and starts swimming for shore.

WIPE TO: INT. TOLL HOUSE ON BRIDGE—NIGHT

MED. SHOT—George, Clarence, and the tollkeeper. George is seated before a wood burning stove before which his clothes are drying on a line. He is in his long winter underwear. He is sipping a mug of hot coffee, staring at the stove, cold, gloomy and drunk, ignoring Clarence and the tollkeeper, preoccupied by his near suicide and his unsolved problems. Clarence is standing on the other side of the stove, putting on his undershirt. This is a ludicrous seventeenth century garment which looks like a baby's night shirt—with embroidered cuffs and collar, and gathered at the neck with a drawstring. It falls below his knees.

The tollkeeper is seated against the wall eyeing them suspiciously. Throughout the scene he attempts to spit, but each time is stopped by some amazing thing Clarence does or says. Clarence becomes aware that his garment is amazing the tollkeeper.

CLARENCE: I didn't have time to get some stylish underwear. My wife gave me this on my last birthday. I passed away in it.

The tollkeeper, about to spit, is stopped in the middle of it by this remark. Clarence, secretly trying to get George's attention, now picks up a copy of "Tom Sawyer" which is hanging on the line, drying. He shakes the book.

CLARENCE (cont'd): Oh, Tom Sawyer's drying out, too. You should read the new book Mark Twain's writing now.

The tollkeeper stares at him incredulously.

TOLLKEEPER: How'd you happen to fall in?

CLARENCE: I didn't fall in. I jumped in to save George.

George looks up, surprised.

GEORGE: You what? To save me?

CLARENCE: Well, I did, didn't I? You didn't go through with it, did you?

GEORGE: Go through with what?

CLARENCE: Suicide.

George and the tollkeeper react to this.

TOLLKEEPER: It's against the law to commit suicide around here.

CLARENCE: Yeah, it's against the law where I come from, too.

TOLLKEEPER: Where do you come from?

He leans forward to spit, but is stopped by Clarence's next statement.

CLARENCE: Heaven.
    (to George)
I had to act quickly, that's why I jumped in. I knew if I were drowning you'd try to save me. And you see, you did, and that's how I saved you.

The tollkeeper becomes increasingly nervous. George casually looks at the strange smiling little man a second time.

GEORGE (off hand): Very funny.

CLARENCE: Your lip's bleeding, George.

George's hand goes to his mouth.

GEORGE: Yeah, I got a bust in the jaw in answer to a prayer a little bit ago.

CLARENCE: (comes around to George) Oh, no—no—no, George. I'm the answer to your prayer. That's why I was sent down here.

GEORGE (casually interested): How do you know my name.

CLARENCE: Oh, I know all about you. I've watched you grow up from a little boy.

GEORGE: What are you, a mind reader or something?

CLARENCE: Oh, no.

GEORGE: Well, who are you, then?

CLARENCE: Clarence Odbody, A-S-2.

GEORGE: Odbody . . . A-S-2. What's that A-S-2?

CLARENCE: Angel Second Class.

❋

The tollkeeper's chair slips out from under him with a crash. He has been leaning against the wall on it, tipped back on two legs. Tollkeeper rises and makes his way warily out the door. From his expression he looks like he'll call the nearest cop.

CLARENCE (cont'd, to tollkeeper): Cheerio, my good man.

George rubs his head with his hand, to clear his mind.

GEORGE: Oh, brother. I wonder what Martini put in those drinks?

He looks up at Clarence standing beside him.

GEORGE (cont'd): Hey, what's with you? What did you say just a minute ago? Why'd you want to save me?

CLARENCE: That's what I was sent down for. I'm your guardian angel.

GEORGE: I wouldn't be a bit surprised.

CLARENCE: Ridiculous of you to think of killing yourself for money. Eight thousand dollars.

GEORGE (bewildered): Yeah . . . just things like that. Now how'd you know that?

CLARENCE: I told you—I'm your guardian angel. I know everything about you.

GEORGE: Well, you look about like the kind of an angel

I'd get. Sort of a fallen angel, aren't you? What happened to your wings.

CLARENCE: I haven't won my wings yet. That's why I'm an Angel Second Class.

GEORGE: I don't know whether I like it very much being seen around with an angel without any wings.

CLARENCE: Oh, I've got to earn them, and you'll help me, won't you?

GEORGE (humoring him): Sure, sure. How?

CLARENCE: By letting me help you.

GEORGE: Only one way you can help me. You don't happen to have eight thousand bucks on you?

CLARENCE: Oh, no, no. We don't use money in Heaven.

GEORGE: Oh, that's right, I keep forgetting. Comes in pretty handy down here, bub.

CLARENCE: Oh, tut, tut, tut.

GEORGE: I found it out a little late. I'm worth more dead than alive.

CLARENCE: Now look, you mustn't talk like that. I won't get my wings with that attitude. You just don't know all that you've done. If it hadn't been for you....

✳

GEORGE (interrupts): Yeah, if it hadn't been for me, everybody'd be a lot better off. My wife, and my kids and my friends. (Annoyed with Clarence) Look, little fellow, go off and haunt somebody else, will you?

CLARENCE: No, you don't understand. I've got my job. . . .

GEORGE (savagely): Aw, shut up, will you.

Clarence is not getting far with George. He glances up, paces across the room, thoughtfully.

CLARENCE (to himself): Hmmm, this isn't going to be so easy. (To George) So you still think killing yourself would make everyone feel happier, eh?

GEORGE (dejectedly): Oh, I don't know. I guess you're right. I suppose it would have been better if I'd never been born at all.

CLARENCE: What'd you say?

GEORGE: I said I wish I'd never been born.

CLARENCE: Oh, you mustn't say things like that. You . . . (gets an idea) . . . wait a minute. Wait a minute. That's an idea. (Glances up toward Heaven) What do *you* think? Yeah, that'll do it. All right. (To George) You've got your wish. You've never been born.

As Clarence speaks this line, the snow stops falling outside the building, a strong wind springs up which blows open the door to the shack. Clarence runs to close the door.

CLARENCE (cont'd, looking upward):You don't have to make all that fuss about it.

As Clarence speaks, George cocks his head curiously, favoring his deaf ear, more interested in this hearing than in what Clarence has said.

GEORGE: What did you say?

CLARENCE: You've never been born. You don't exist. You haven't a care in the world.

George feels his ear as Clarence talks.

CLARENCE (cont'd): No worries—no obligations—no eight thousand dollars to get—no Potter looking for you with the Sheriff.

CLOSEUP—George and Clarence. George indicates his bad ear.

GEORGE: Say something else in that ear.

CLARENCE (bending down): Sure. You can hear out of it.

GEORGE: Well, that's the doggonedest thing . . . I haven't heard anything out of that ear since I was a kid. Must have been that jump in the cold water.

CLARENCE: Your lip's stopped bleeding, too, George.

✳

George feels his lip, which shows no sign of the recent cut he received from Welch. He is now thoroughly confused.

GEORGE: What do you know about that . . . What's happened?

MED. CLOSE SHOT—George looks around, as though to get his bearings.

GEORGE: It's stopped snowing out, hasn't it? What's happened here? (Standing up) Come on, soon as these clothes of ours are dry....

CLARENCE: Our clothes *are* dry.

George feels the clothes on the line.

GEORGE: What do you know about that? Stove's hotter than I thought. Now, come on, get your clothes on, and we'll stroll up to my car and get. ...

They start dressing. George interrupts himself.

GEORGE (cont'd): Oh, I'm sorry. I'll stroll. You fly.

CLARENCE: I can't fly. I haven't got my wings.

GEORGE: You haven't got your wings. Yeah, that's right.

WIPE TO: EXT. STREET—NIGHT

MED. SHOT—This is the same empty street where

George's car swerved into the tree near the sidewalk. George and Clarence come into shot and up to the spot where George had left his car smashed against the tree. George looks around, but his car is nowhere to be seen, and the tree is undamaged.

CLARENCE: What's the matter?

GEORGE (puzzled): Well, this is where I left my car and it isn't here.

CLARENCE: You have no car.

GEORGE: Well, I had a car, and it was right here. I guess somebody moved it.

CLOSE SHOT—at curb. The owner of the house passes with some Christmas packages under his arm.

OWNER (politely): Good evening.

GEORGE: Oh, say . . . Hey . . . where's my car?

OWNER: I beg your pardon?

GEORGE: My car, my car. I'm the fellow that owns the car that ran into your tree.

OWNER: What tree?

GEORGE: What do you mean, what tree? This tree. Here, I ran into it. Cut a big gash in the side of it here.

The owner bends down to examine the trunk of the tree, then straightens up and smells George's breath. He backs away.

OWNER: You must mean two other trees. You had me worried. One of the oldest trees in Pottersville.

GEORGE (blankly): Pottersville? Why, you mean Bedford Falls.

OWNER: I mean Pottersville. (Sharply) Don't you think I know where I live? What's the matter with you?

The owner proceeds toward his house. George is completely bewildered.

GEORGE: Oh, I don't know. Either I'm off my nut, or he is . . . (to Clarence) or you are!

CLARENCE: It isn't me!

GEORGE: Well, maybe I left the car up at Martini's. Well, come on, Gabriel.

He puts his arm around Clarence, and they start off up the road.

CLARENCE (as they go): Clarence!

GEORGE: Clarence! Clarence!

WIPE TO: INT. NICK'S BAR—NIGHT

CLOSE SHOT—It is Martini's place, but almost unrecognizable. The cheerful Italian feeling is gone. It is now more of a hard-drinking joint, a honky-tonk. Same bar, tables have no covers. People are lower down and tougher. Nick the bartender is behind the bar. George and Clarence come in. George does not notice the difference, but Clarence is all eyes and beaming. They go up to the bar.

GEORGE (as they come in): That's all right. Go on in. Martini's a good friend of mine.

Two people leave the bar as they approach.

GEORGE (cont'd): There's a place to sit down. Sit down.

MED. CLOSEUP—Nick is wiping off the bar as they sit down.

GEORGE (cont'd): Oh, hello, Nick. Hey, where's Martini?

NICK: You want a martini?

GEORGE: No, no, Martini. Your boss. Where is he?

NICK (impatient): Look, I'm the boss. You want a drink or don't you?

GEORGE: Okay—all right. Double bourbon, quick, huh?

NICK: Okay. (To Clarence) What's yours?

CLARENCE: I was just thinking.... (face puckers up

✳

with delicious anticipation) It's been so long since I....

NICK (impatient): Look, mister, I'm standing here waiting for you to make up your mind.

CLARENCE (appreciatively): That's a good man. I was just thinking of a flaming rum punch. No, it's not cold enough for that. Not nearly cold enough.... Wait a minute.... wait a minute. ... I got it. Mulled wine, heavy on the cinnamon and light on the cloves. Off with you, me lad, and belively!

NICK: Hey, look mister, we serve hard drinks in here for men who want to get drunk fast. And we don't need any characters around to give the joint atmosphere. Is that clear? Or do I have to slip you my left for a convincer?

As he says this, Nick leans over the counter, and puts his left fist nearly in Clarence's eye. Clarence is puzzled by this conduct.

CLARENCE (to George): What's he talking about?

GEORGE (soothingly): Nick—Nick, just give him the same as mine. He's okay.

NICK: Okay.

Nick turns away to get the drinks.

GEORGE: What's the matter with him? I never saw

Nick act like that before.

CLARENCE: You'll see a lot of strange things from now on.

GEORGE: Oh, yeah. Hey, little fellow—you worry me. You got someplace to sleep?

CLARENCE: No.

GEORGE: You don't, huh? Well, you got any money?

Nick is listening suspiciously to this conversation.

CLARENCE: No.

GEORGE: No wonder you jumped in the river.

CLARENCE: I jumped in the river to save you so I could get my wings.

Nick stops pouring the drinks, bottle poised in his hand.

GEORGE: Oh, that's right.

A cash register bell rings off stage. Clarence reacts to the SOUND of the bell.

CLARENCE: Oh - oh. Somebody's just made it.

GEORGE: Made what?

CLARENCE: Every time you hear a bell ring, it means

that some angel's just got his wings.

George glances up at Nick.

GEORGE: Look, I think maybe you better not mention getting your wings around here.

CLARENCE: Why? Don't they believe in angels?

GEORGE (looking at Nick): A ... Yeah, but ... you know ...

CLARENCE: Then why should they be surprised when they see one?

GEORGE (to Nick): He never grew up. He's.... (to Clarence) How old are you, anyway, Clarence?

CLARENCE: Two hundred and ninety-three.... (thinks) ... next May.

Nick slams the bottle down on the counter.

NICK: That does it! Out you two pixies go, through the door or out the window!

GEORGE: Look, Nick. What's wrong?

NICK (angrily): And that's another thing. Where do *you* come off calling me Nick?

GEORGE: Well, Nick, that's your name, isn't it?

NICK: What's that got to do with it? I don't know you from Adam's off ox. (Sees someone come in) Hey, you!

Rummy! Come here! Come here!

CLOSE SHOT—a small wreck of a man, with weak, watery eyes. Obviously a broken-down panhandler, his hat in his hand.

CLOSEUP—George. He can hardly believe his eyes. It is Gower, the druggist.

BACK TO SHOT—Nick at the bar.

NICK (to Gower): Didn't I tell you never to come panhandling around here?

Nick picks up a seltzer bottle, and squirts Gower in the face with it. The crowd laughs brutally. Gower smiles weakly, as the soda runs off his face.

CLOSE SHOT—George, horrified, leaps up and goes over to Gower.

GEORGE: Mr. Gower! Mr. Gower! This is George Bailey! Don't you know me?

GOWER: No. No.

NICK (to his bouncers): Throw him out. Throw him out.

The bouncers throw Gower out the front door. George rushes back to the bar.

GEORGE (bewildered): Hey, what is. . . . Hey, Nick, Nick. . . . Isn't that Mr. Gower, the druggist?

✳

NICK: You know, that's another reason for me not to like you. That rum-head spent twenty years in jail for poisoning a kid. If you know him, you must be a jail-bird yourself. (To his bouncers) Would you show these gentlemen to the door.

BOUNCER: Sure. This way, gentlemen.

EXT. NICK'S BAR—NIGHT

CLOSE SHOT—George and Clarence come flying through the door and land in the snow.

INT. NICK'S BAR—NIGHT

CLOSE SHOT—Nick at the cash register, busily ringing the bell.

NICK: Hey! Get me! I'm giving out wings!

EXT. NICK'S BAR—NIGHT

CLOSE SHOT—George and Clarence lying in the snow. George has a strange, puzzled look on his face. They remain for a moment as they landed, looking at each other.

CLARENCE: You see, George, you were not there to stop Gower from putting that poison into the....

GEORGE: What do you mean, I wasn't there? I remember distinctly ...

George catches a glimpse of the front of the building

with the neon sign over the door. It now reads "NICK'S PLACE" instead of "MARTINI'S."

George and Clarence get to their feet.

GEORGE (exasperated): What the.... hey, what's going on around here? Why, this ought to be Martini's place.

He points to the sign, and looks at Clarence. Clarence sort of hangs his head. George fixes him with a very interested look.

GEORGE (cont'd): Look, who are you?

CLARENCE (patiently): I told you, George. I'm your guardian angel.

George, still looking at him, goes up to him and pokes his arm. It's flesh.

GEORGE: Yeah, yeah, I know. You told me that. What else are you? What...are you a hypnotist?

CLARENCE: No, of course not.

GEORGE: Well then, why am I seeing all these strange things?

CLARENCE: Don't you understand, George? It's because you were not born.

GEORGE: Then if I wasn't born, who am I?

CLARENCE: You're nobody. You have no identity.

George rapidly searches his pockets for identification, but without success.

GEORGE: What do you mean, no identity? My name's George Bailey.

CLARENCE: There is no George Bailey. You have no papers, no cards, no driver's license, no 4-F card, no insurance policy . . . (he says these things as George searches for them)

George looks in his watch pocket.

CLARENCE (cont'd) : They're not there, either.

GEORGE: What?

CLARENCE: Zuzu's petals.

George feverishly continues to turn his pockets inside out.

CLARENCE (cont'd): You've been given a great gift, George. A chance to see what the world would be like without you.

George is completely befuddled.

GEORGE (shaking his head): Now wait a minute, here. Wait a minute here. Aw, this is some sort of funny dream I'm having here. So long, mister, I'm going home.

He starts off. Clarence rises.

CLARENCE: Home? What home?

GEORGE (furious): Now shut up! Cut it out! You're . . . you're . . . you're crazy! That's what I think . . . you're screwy, and you're driving me crazy, too! I'm seeing things. I'm going home and see my wife and family. Do you understand that? And I'm going home alone!

George strides off hurriedly. Clarence slowly follows him, glancing up toward Heaven as he goes.

CLARENCE: How'm I doing, Joseph? Thanks. (Pause) No, I didn't have a drink!

WIPE TO: EXT. STREET—NIGHT

MED. SHOT—George moves into the scene. The sign bearing the name of the town reads: "POTTERSVILLE." George looks at it in surprise, then starts up the street toward the main part of town. As he goes, CAMERA MOVES WITH him. The character of the place has completely changed. Where before it was a quiet, orderly small town, it has now become in nature like a frontier village. We see a SERIES OF SHOTS of night clubs, cafes, bars, liquor stores, pool halls and the like, with blaring jazz MUSIC issuing from the majority of them. The motion picture theatre has become a burlesque house, Gower's drug store is now a pawnbroker's establishment, and so on.

CLOSE SHOT—George stops before what used to be

the offices of the Building and Loan. There is a garish electric sign over the entrance reading: "Welcome Jitterbugs." A crowd of people are watching the police, who are raiding the place, and dragging out a number of screaming women, whom they throw into a patrol wagon. George talks to one of the cops:

GEORGE: Hey . . . hey. Where did the Building and Loan move to?

COP: The Building and what?

GEORGE: The Bailey Building and Loan. It was up there.

COP: They went out of business years ago.

MED. CLOSEUP—George sees the struggling figure of Violet Bick, arrayed as a tart, being dragged into the patrol wagon.

GEORGE: Hey, Violet! (to the cop) Hey, listen—that's Violet Bick!

COP: I know. I know.

GEORGE: I know that girl!

The cop shoves George to one side. He looks around and sees Ernie's taxi cruising slowly by.

GEORGE (cont'd): Hey, Ernie—Ernie!

EXT. STREET—NIGHT

CLOSE SHOT—Ernie stops the cab, and George enters it.

GEORGE: Ernie, take me home. I'm off my nut!

ERNIE (a much harder Ernie): Where do you live?

GEORGE: Aw, now, doggone it, Ernie, don't you start pulling that stuff. You know where I live. Three-twenty Sycamore. Now hurry up.

ERNIE: Okay. Three-twenty Sycamore? . . .

GEORGE: Yeah—yeah—hurry up. Zuzu's sick.

ERNIE: All right.

He pulls down the flag on the meter and starts the cab.

INT. CAB—NIGHT

MED. CLOSEUP—George and Ernie. Ernie is puzzled by the stranger.

GEORGE: Look here, Ernie, straighten me out here. I've got some bad liquor or something. Listen to me now. Now, you are Ernie Bishop, and you live in Bailey Park with your wife and kid? That's right, isn't it?

ERNIE (suspiciously): You seen my wife?

GEORGE (exasperated): Seen your wife! I've been to your house a hundred times.

ERNIE: Look, bud, what's the idea? I live in a shack in Potter's Field and my wife ran away three years ago and took the kid.... And I ain't never seen you before in my life.

GEORGE: Okay. Just step on it. Just get me home.

Ernie turns to driving, but he's worried about his passenger. As he passes the burlesque house he sees Bert the cop standing beside his police car. Attracting his attention, he motions to Bert to follow him, indicating he has a nut in the back. Bert gets into his car and follows.

WIPE TO: EXT. GEORGE'S HOUSE—NIGHT

MED. LONG SHOT—The taxi pulls up to the curb and stops.

MED. CLOSE SHOT—The cab is parked. George gets out and looks at the house.

ERNIE: Is this the place?

GEORGE: Of course it's the place.

ERNIE: Well, this house ain't been lived in for twenty years.

EXT. HOUSE—NIGHT

MED. SHOT—George is stopped momentarily by the appearance of the house. Windows are broken, the porch sags, one section of the roof has fallen, doors and shutters hang askew on their hinges. Like a doomed man, George approaches the house.

EXT. CAB—NIGHT

MED. CLOSE SHOT—The police car has pulled up beside the cab, and Bert and Ernie stand watching George's actions.

BERT: What's up, Ernie?

ERNIE: I don't know, but we better keep an eye on this guy. He's bats.

Ernie switches on the spotlight on his cab, and turns the beam toward the old house.

INT. HALLWAY GEORGE'S HOUSE—NIGHT

CLOSE SHOT—The interior of the house is lit up here and there, ghostlike, by Ernie's spotlight. No furniture, cobwebs, wallpaper hanging and swinging—stairs are broken and collapsed. In a voice that sounds like a cry for help, George yells out:

GEORGE: Mary! Mary! Tommy! Pete! Janie! Zuzu! Where are you?

Clarence suddenly appears leaning against a wall.

CLARENCE: They're not here, George. You have no children.

GEORGE (ignoring him): Where are you? (then to Clarence) What have you done with them?

INT. DOORWAY—NIGHT

CLOSE SHOT—Bert is standing in the entrance, with his gun in his hand. Ernie is a few feet behind him, ready to run.

BERT: All right, put up your hands. No fast moves. Come on out here, both of you.

GEORGE: Bert! Thank heaven you're here!

He rushes toward Bert.

BERT: Stand back!

GEORGE: Bert, what's happened to this house? Where's Mary? Where's my kids?

ERNIE (warningly): Watch him, Bert.

BERT: Come on, come on.

GEORGE (bewildered): Bert—Ernie! What's the matter with you two guys? You were here on my wedding night. You, both of you, stood out here on the porch and sung to us, don't you remember?

ERNIE (nervously): Think I'd better be going.

BERT: Look, now why don't you be a good kid and we'll

✳

take you into a doctor. Everything's going to be all right.

Bert tries to lead George away by the arm, but George struggles with him, trying to explain.

GEORGE: Bert, now listen to me. Ernie, will you take me over to my mother's house? Bert, listen! (gesturing to Clarence) It's that fellow there—he says he's an angel— he's tried to hypnotize me.

BERT: I hate to do this, fella.

Bert raises his gun to hit George on the head. As he does so, Clarence darts in and fixes his teeth in Bert's wrist, forcing him to let George go.

CLARENCE: Run … George! Run, George!

George dashes out of the house, and down the street, as Bert grapples with Clarence, and they fall to the ground, wrestling. We see Bert kneeling, trying to put handcuffs on Clarence.

CLARENCE (cont'd): Help! Joseph, help!

BERT: Oh, shut up!

CLARENCE: Help, Oh Joseph, help! Joseph!

Suddenly Clarence disappears from under Bert's hands. Bert gets up, amazed by his vanishing.

BERT: Where'd he go? Where'd he go? I had him right here.

Ernie's hair is now standing on end with fright.

ERNIE (stammering): I need a drink.

He runs out of the scene.

BERT: Well, which way'd they go? Help me find 'em.

EXT. BAILEY HOME—NIGHT

MED. SHOT—George runs up the path to the front door of the house, and raps on the door. He rings the bell and taps on the glass, when his attention is caught by a sign on the wall reading: "Ma Bailey's Boarding House."

MED. CLOSEUP—George at the door. The door opens and a woman appears. It is Mrs. Bailey, but she has changed amazingly. Her face is harsh and tired. In her eyes, once kindly and understanding, there is now cold suspicion. She gives no sign that she knows him.

MA BAILEY: Well?

GEORGE: Mother....

MA BAILEY: Mother? What do you want?

It is a cruel blow to George.

GEORGE: Mother, this is George. I thought sure you'd remember me.

MA BAILEY (coldly): George who? If you're looking for a room there's no vacancy.

She starts to close the door, but George stops her.

GEORGE: Oh, mother, mother, please help me. Something terrible's happened to me. I don't know what it is. Something's happened to everybody. Please let me come in. Keep me here until I get over it.

MA BAILEY: Get over what? I don't take in strangers unless they're sent here by somebody I know.

GEORGE (desperate): Well, I know everybody you know. Your brother-in-law, Uncle Billy.

MA BAILEY (suspiciously): You know him?

GEORGE: Well, sure I do.

MA BAILEY: When'd you see him last?

GEORGE: Today, over at his house.

MA BAILEY: That's a lie. He's been in the insane asylum ever since he lost his business. And if you ask me, that's where you belong.

She slams the door shut in George's face.

EXT. HOUSE—NIGHT

MED. CLOSE SHOT—George stands a moment,

stunned. Then he turns and runs out to the sidewalk, until his face fills the screen. His features are distorted by the emotional chaos within him. We see Clarence leaning on the mail box at the curb, holding his volume of "Tom Sawyer" in his hand.

CLARENCE: Strange, isn't it? Each man's life touches so many other lives, and when he isn't around he leaves an awful hole, doesn't he?

GEORGE (quietly, trying to use logic): I've heard of things like this. You've got me in some kind of a spell, or something. Well, I'm going to get out of it. I'll get out of it. I know how, too. I . . . the last man I talked to before all this stuff started happening to me was Martini.

CLARENCE: You know where he lives?

GEORGE: Sure I know where he lives. He lives in Bailey Park.

They walk out of scene.

WIPE TO: EXT. CEMETERY—NIGHT

MED. SHOT—George and Clarence approach the tree from which the "Bailey Park" sign once hung. Now it is just outside a cemetery, with graves where the houses used to be.

CLARENCE: Are you sure this is Bailey Park?

GEORGE: Oh, I'm not sure of anything anymore. All I know is this should be Bailey Park. But where are the houses?

The two walk into the cemetery.

CLARENCE (as they go): You weren't here to build them.

CLOSE MOVING SHOT—George wandering like a lost soul among the tombstones, Clarence trotting at his heels. Again George stops to stare with frightened eyes at:

CLOSE SHOT—a tombstone. Upon it is engraved a name, Harry Bailey. Feverishly George scrapes away the snow covering the rest of the inscription, and we read: IN MEMORY OF OUR BELOVED SON—HARRY BAILEY—1911—1919.

CLOSE SHOT—George and Clarence.

CLARENCE: Your brother, Harry Bailey, broke through the ice and was drowned at the age of nine.

George jumps up.

GEORGE: That's a lie! Harry Bailey went to war! He got the Congressional Medal of Honor! He saved the lives of every man on that transport.

CLARENCE (sadly): Every man on that transport died. Harry wasn't there to save them because you weren't there to save Harry. You see, George, you really had a wonderful life. Don't you see what a mistake it would be to throw it away?

CLOSEUP—George and Clarence

GEORGE: Clarence …

CLARENCE: Yes, George?

GEORGE: Where's Mary?

CLARENCE: Oh, well, I can't …

GEORGE: I don't know how you know these things, but tell me—where is she?

George grabs Clarence by the coat collar and shakes him.

CLARENCE: I …

GEORGE: If you know where she is, tell me where my wife is.

CLARENCE: I'm not supposed to tell.

GEORGE (becoming violent): Please, Clarence, tell me where she is.

CLARENCE: You're not going to like it, George.

GEORGE (shouting): Where is she?

CLARENCE: She's an old maid. She never married.

GEORGE (choking him): Where's Mary? Where is she?

CLARENCE: She's. . . .

GEORGE: Where is she?

CLARENCE (in self defense): She's just about to close up the library!

George lets Clarence go, and runs off. Clarence falls to the ground, where he rubs his neck.

CLARENCE (to himself): There must be some easier way for me to get my wings.

EXT. LIBRARY—NIGHT

CLOSE SHOT—Mary comes out the door, then turns and locks it. We see George watching her from the sidewalk. Mary is very different—no buoyancy in her walk, none of Mary's abandon and love of life. Glasses, no make-up, lips compressed, elbows close to body. She looks flat and dried up, and extremely self-satisfied and efficient.

CLOSEUP—George, as he watches her.

CLOSE SHOT—George and Mary, on the sidewalk.

GEORGE: Mary!

She looks up, surprised, but, not recognizing him, continues on.

GEORGE (cont'd): Mary!

Mary starts to run away from him, and he follows, desperately.

GEORGE (cont'd): Mary! Mary!

He catches up to her, grabs her by the arms, and keeps a tight grip on her. She struggles to free herself.

GEORGE (cont'd): Mary, it's George! Don't you know me? What's happened to us?

MARY (struggling): I don't know you! Let me go!

GEORGE: Mary, please! Oh, don't do this to me. Please, Mary, help me. Where's our kids? I need you, Mary! Help me, Mary!

Mary breaks away from him, and dashes into the first door she comes to, the Blue Moon Bar.

INT. BLUE MOON—NIGHT

CLOSE SHOT—Small tables, booths, perhaps a counter. It is crowded. Many of the people are the same who were present during the run on the Building and Loan. Mary comes running in, screaming. The place goes into an uproar. George comes in, practically insane. Some of the men grab and hold on to him.

GEORGE (shouting): Mary. . . . (to men holding him) Let

me go! Mary, don't run away!

MAN: Somebody call the police!

ANOTHER MAN: Hit him with a bottle!

ANOTHER MAN: He needs a straight jacket!

MARY (from back of room): That man—stop him!

GEORGE (recognizing some of them): Tom! Ed! Charlie! That's my wife!

Mary lets out a final scream, then faints into the arms of a couple of women at the bar.

GEORGE (cont'd): Mary!

MAN: Oh, no you don't!

GEORGE (screaming): Mary!

George can't fight through the men holding him. Desperately he thinks of Clarence, and heads for the door.

GEORGE (cont'd): Clarence! Clarence! Where are you?

EXT. SIDEWALK—NIGHT

CLOSE SHOT—Just as George breaks through the door, Bert arrives in his police car. He gets out and heads for the door, to run into George as he comes out.

BERT: Oh, it's you!

❋

He grabs for George, who lets him have one square on the button, knocking him down, then continues running down the street yelling for Clarence. Bert gets up, takes out his gun and fires several shots after the fleeing figure.

BERT (to crowd): Stand back!

Bert gets into the police car, and, siren screaming, sets off in pursuit of George.

WIPE TO: EXT. BRIDGE OVER RIVER—NIGHT

MED. SHOT—The same part of the bridge where George was standing before Clarence jumped in. The wind is blowing as it has all through this sequence. George comes running into shot. He is frantically looking for Clarence.

GEORGE: Clarence! Clarence! Help me, Clarence. Get me back. Get me back. I don't care what happens to me. Only get me back to my wife and kids. Help me, Clarence, please. Please! I want to live again!

CLOSEUP—George leaning on the bridge railing, praying.

GEORGE: I want to live again. I want to live again. Please, God, let me live again.

George sobs. Suddenly, toward the end of the above, the wind dies down. A soft, gentle snow begins to fall.

CLOSE SHOT—George sobbing at the railing. The police car pulls up on the roadway behind him, and Bert comes into scene.

BERT: Hey, George! George! You all right?

George backs away and gets set to hit Bert again.

BERT (cont'd): Hey, what's the matter?

GEORGE (warningly): Now get out of here, Bert, or I'll hit you again! Get out!

BERT: What the Sam Hill you yelling for, George?

GEORGE: Don't … George?

George talks hopefully—George touches Bert unbelievingly—George's mouth is bleeding again.

GEORGE (cont'd): Bert, do you know me?

BERT: Know you? Are you kiddin'? I've been looking all over town trying to find you. I saw your car piled into that tree down there, and I thought maybe…. Hey, your mouth's bleeding, are you sure you're all right?

GEORGE: What did …

George touches his lips with his tongue, wipes his mouth with his hand, laughs happily. His rapture knows no bounds.

GEORGE (cont'd, joyously): My mouth's bleeding, Bert! My mouth's bleed . . . (feeling in watch pocket) Zuzu's petals! Zuzu's . . . they're . . . they're here Bert! What do you know about that! Merry Christmas!

He practically embraces the astonished Bert, then runs at top speed toward town.

LONG SHOT—George runs away from camera yelling:

GEORGE: Mary! Mary!

WIPE TO: EXT. RESIDENTIAL STREET—NIGHT

CLOSE SHOT—George's wrecked car is smashed against the tree. He comes running into shot, sees the car, let's out a triumphant yell, pets the car, and dashes on.

EXT. MAIN STREET BEDFORD FALLS—NIGHT

CLOSE SHOT—George sees that the POTTERSVILLE sign is now replaced by the original YOU ARE NOW IN BEDFORD FALLS sign.

GEORGE: Hello, Bedford Falls!

He turns and runs through the falling snow up the main street of town. As he runs, he notices that the town is back in its original appearance. He passes some late shoppers on the street:

GEORGE (cont'd): Merry Christmas!

PEOPLE (ad lib): Merry Christmas! Merry Christmas, George!

EXT. THEATRE—NIGHT

PAN SHOT—As George runs by:

GEORGE: Merry Christmas, movie house!

EXT. BEDFORD FALLS EMPORIUM—NIGHT

PAN SHOT—As George runs by:

GEORGE: Merry Christmas, emporium!

EXT. BUILDING AND LOAN OFFICES—NIGHT

PAN SHOT—As George runs by:

GEORGE: Merry Christmas, you wonderful old Building and Loan!

EXT. BANK—NIGHT

CLOSE SHOT—George notices a light in Potter's office window, and races across the street.

INT. POTTER'S OFFICE—NIGHT

CLOSE SHOT—Potter is seated working at his desk, his goon by his side. George pounds on the window.

GEORGE (from outside): Merry Christmas, Mr. Potter!

George runs off as Potter looks up from his work.

POTTER: Happy New Year to you—in jail! Go on home—they're waiting for you!

INT. GEORGE'S HOME—NIGHT

The lights are on. There is a fire in the fireplace. The Christmas tree is fully decorated with presents stacked around.

INT. ENTRANCE HALL—NIGHT

CLOSE SHOT—Carter, the bank examiner, a newspaper reporter and photographer, and a sheriff, are waiting in the hall for George. George comes dashing in the front door.

GEORGE (excitedly): Mary . . . (sees the men) Well, hello, Mr. Bank Examiner!

He grabs his hand and shakes it.

CARTER (surprised): Mr. Bailey, there's a deficit!

GEORGE: I know. Eight thousand dollars.

SHERIFF (reaching in coat): George, I've got a little paper here.

GEORGE (happily): I'll bet it's a warrant for my arrest. Isn't it wonderful? Merry Christmas!

The photographer sets off a flash bulb.

GEORGE: Reporters? Where's Mary? (calling) Mary!

George runs to the kitchen. He gets no answer. As he goes:

GEORGE (cont'd): Oh, look at this wonderful old drafty house! Mary! Mary!

He comes running back to the hall.

GEORGE (cont'd):Have you seen my wife?

CHILDREN'S VOICES: Merry Christmas, daddy! Merry Christmas, daddy!

INT. STAIRS—NIGHT

MED. SHOT—The three children are standing at the top of the stairs. They are in their pajamas.

GEORGE (cont'd): Kids!

George starts to run up the stairs, and the old familiar knob on the bannister comes off in his hand. He kisses it lovingly and puts it back, then continues up the stairs.

GEORGE (cont'd): Pete—kids—Janie—Tommy. (takes them in his arms) I could eat you up!

INT. TOP OF STAIRS—NIGHT

CLOSE SHOT—George and the kids. He is hugging them.

GEORGE: Where's your mother?

JANIE: She went looking for you with Uncle Billy.

Zuzu comes running out of her bedroom. George crushes her to him.

ZUZU: Daddy!

GEORGE: Zuzu—Zuzu. My little gingersnap! How do you feel?

ZUZU: Fine.

JANIE: And not a smitch of temperature.

GEORGE (laughing): Not a smitch of temp . . .

INT. HALL—NIGHT

CLOSE SHOT—As Mary comes through the door, breathless and excited. The four men are watching with open mouths.

GEORGE'S VOICE: Hallelujah!

MARY (to the men): Hello. (sees George) George! Darling!

INT. STAIRS—NIGHT

CLOSE SHOT—Mary races up the stairs, where George meets her in a fierce embrace.

GEORGE: Mary! Mary!

MARY: George, darling! Where have you been?

George and Mary embrace tearfully.

MARY (cont'd): Oh, George, George, George.

GEORGE: Mary! Let me touch you! Oh, you're real!

MARY: Oh, George, George!

GEORGE: You have no idea what's happened to me.

MARY: You have no idea what happened . . .

He stops her with a kiss. She leads him excitedly down the stairs.

MARY (cont'd): Well, come on, George, come on down-stairs quick. They're on their way.

GEORGE: All right.

INT. LIVING ROOM—NIGHT

CLOSE SHOT—Mary leads George, who is carrying a couple of the kids on his back, to a position in front of the Christmas tree.

MARY: Come on in here now. Now, you stand right over here, by the tree. Right there, and don't move, don't move. I hear 'em now, George, it's a miracle! It's a miracle!

She runs toward front door and flings it open. Ad lib SOUNDS of an excited crowd can be heard. Uncle Billy, face flushed, covered with snow, and carrying a clothes basket filled with money, bursts in. He is followed by Ernie, and about twenty more townspeople.

MARY: Come in, Uncle Billy! Everybody! In here!

Uncle Billy, Mary and the crowd come into the living room. A table stands in front of George. George picks up Zuzu to protect her from the mob. Uncle Billy dumps the basketful of money out onto the table—the money overflows and falls all over.

UNCLE BILLY: Isn't it wonderful?

The rest of the crowd all greet George with greetings and smiles. Each one comes forward with money. In their pockets, in shoe boxes, in coffee pots. Money pours onto the table—pennies, dimes, quarters, dollar bills—small money, but lots of it. Mrs. Bailey and Mrs. Hatch push toward George. More people come in. The place becomes a bedlam. Shouts of "Gangway—gangway" as a new bunch comes in and pours out its money. Mary stands next to George, watching him. George stands there overcome and speechless as he holds Zuzu. As he sees the familiar faces, he gives them sick grins. Tears course down his face. His lips frame their names as he greets them.

UNCLE BILLY (cont'd, emotionally at the breaking point): Mary did it, George! Mary did it! She told a few people you were in trouble and they scattered all over town collecting money. They didn't ask any questions— just said: "If George is in trouble—count on me." You never saw anything like it.

Tom comes in, digging in his purse as he comes.

TOM: What is this, George? Another run on the bank?

Charlie adds his money to the pile.

CHARLIE: Here you are, George. Merry Christmas.

Ernie is trying to get some system into the chaos.

ERNIE: The line forms on the right.

Mr. Martini comes in bearing a mixing bowl overflowing with cash.

ERNIE (cont'd): Mr. Martini! Merry Christmas! Step right up here.

Martini dumps his money on the table.

MARTINI: I busted the juke-box, too!

Mr. Gower enters with a large glass jar jammed full of notes.

ERNIE: Mr. Gower!

GOWER (to George): I made the rounds of my charge accounts.

Violet Bick arrives, and takes out the money George had given her for her trip to New York.

GEORGE: Violet Bick!

VIOLET: I'm not going to go, George. I changed my mind.

Annie, the colored maid enters, digging money out of a long black stocking.

ANNIE: I've been saving this money for a divorce, if ever I get a husband.

Mr. Partridge, the high school principal, is the next donor.

PARTRIDGE: There you are, George. I got the faculty all up out of bed. (Hands his watch to Zuzu) And here's something for you to play with.

MAN (giving money): I wouldn't have a roof over my head if it wasn't for you, George.

Ernie is reading a telegram he has just received.

ERNIE: Just a minute. Quiet, everybody. Quiet—quiet. Now, this is from London. (Reading) Mr. Gower cables you need cash. Stop. My office instructed to advance you up to twenty-five thousand dollars. Stop. Hee-haw and Merry Christmas. Sam Wainwright.

The crowd breaks into a cheer as Ernie drops the telegram on top of the pile of money on the table.

MARY (calling out): Mr. Martini. How about some wine?

As various members of the family bring out a punch bowl and glasses, Janie sits down at the piano and strikes a chord. She starts playing "Hark the Herald Angels Sing," and the entire crowd joins in the singing. We see a SERIES OF SHOTS of the various groups singing the hymn, and some people are still coming in and dropping their money on the table. Carter, the bank examiner, makes a donation, the sheriff sheepishly looks at George and tears his warrant in small pieces. In the midst of this scene, Harry, in Naval uniform, enters, accompanied by Bert, the cop.

HARRY: Hello, George, how are you?

GEORGE: Harry ... Harry ...

HARRY (as he sees the money): Mary—looks like I got here too late.

BERT: Mary, I got him here from the airport as quickly as I could. The fool flew all the way up here in a blizzard.

Mrs. Bailey enters scene.

MRS. BAILEY: Harry, how about your banquet in New York?

HARRY: Oh, I left right in the middle of it as soon as I got

❋

Mary's telegram.

Ernie hands Harry a glass of wine.

HARRY (cont'd): Good idea, Ernie. A toast . . . to my big brother, George. The richest man in town!

Once more the crowd breaks into cheering and applause. Janie at the piano and Bert on his accordion, start playing "Auld Lang Syne," and everyone joins in.

CLOSE SHOT—George, still holding Zuzu in his arms, glances down at the pile of money on the table. His eye catches something on top of the pile, and he reaches down for it. It is Clarence's copy of "Tom Sawyer." George opens it and finds an inscription written in it : "Dear George, remember no man is a failure who has friends. Thanks for the wings, Love Clarence."

MARY (looking at book): What's that?

GEORGE: That's a Christmas present from a very dear friend of mine.

At this moment, perhaps because of the jostling of some of the people on the other side of the tree, a little silver bell on the Christmas tree swings to and fro with a silvery tinkle. Zuzu closes the cover of the book, and points to the bell.

ZUZU: Look daddy. Teacher says, every time a bell rings

an angel gets his wings.

GEORGE (smiling): That's right, that's right.

He looks up toward the ceiling and winks.

GEORGE (cont'd): Attaboy, Clarence.

The voices of the people singing swell into a final crescendo for the

FADE OUT

ANNE SEXTON

Christmas Eve

OH SHARP diamond,
my mother!
    I could not count the cost
    of all your faces, your moods—
    that present that I lost.
    Sweet girl, my deathbed,
    my jewel-fingered lady,
    your portrait flickered all night
    by the bulbs of the tree.

Anne Sexton's complex, dark poems alternated between descriptions of madness and intense religious yearning. After publishing Live or Die in 1966, Sexton was awarded the Pulitzer Prize. "Christmas Eve" is from her Complete Poems.

Your face as calm as the moon
over a mannered sea,
presided at the family reunion,
the twelve grandchildren
you used to wear on your wrist,
a three-months-old baby,
a fat check you never wrote,
the red-haired toddler who danced the twist,
your aging daughters, each one a wife,
each one talking to the family cook,
each one avoiding your portrait,
each one aping your life.

Later, after the party,
after the house went to bed,
I sat up drinking the Christmas brandy,
watching your picture,
letting the tree move in and out of focus.
The bulbs vibrated.
They were a halo over your forehead.
Then they were a beehive,
blue, yellow, green, red;
each with its own juice, each hot and alive
stinging your face. But you did not move.
I continued to watch, forcing myself,

❋

waiting, inexhaustible, thirty-five.

I wanted your eyes, like the shadows
of two small birds, to change.
But they did not age.
The smile that gathered me in, all wit,
all charm, was invincible.
Hour after hour I looked at your face
but I could not pull the roots out of it.
Then I watched how the sun hit
your red sweater, your withered neck,
your badly painted flesh-pink skin.
You who led me by the nose,
I saw you as you were.
Then I thought of your body
as one thinks of murder . . .

Then I said Mary—
Mary, Mary, forgive me
and then I touched a present for the child,
the last I bred before your death;
and then I touched my breast
and then I touched the floor
and then my breast again as if,
somehow, it were one of yours.

RAINER MARIA RILKE

Birth of Christ

ADST THOU

not simplicity, how should
> that happen to thee which now lights up the
>> night?
> See, the God who rumbled over nations
> makes himself mild and in thee comes into the
>> world.

---

*The German writer Rainer Maria Rilke fused romantic art,
intense emotions and a mystical relationship with God to create
singular, meticulously crafted poems. "Birth of Christ," from the
Poems of Rainer Maria Rilke (1938), is a perfect example of the
writing that has gained Rilke a substantial following.*

CHRISTMAS STORIES

※

Hadst thou imagined him greater?

What is greatness? Right through all measures
that he crosses goes his straight destiny.
Even a star has no such path,
see thou, these kings are great,

and they drag before thy lap

treasures that they hold to be the greatest,
and thou art perhaps astonished at this gift—:
but look into the folds of thy shawl,
how even now he has exceeded all.

All amber that one ships afar,
all ornament of gold and the aromatic spice
that spreads blurringly in the senses:
all this was of rapid brevity,
and who knows but one has regretted it.

But (thou wilt see): He brings joy.

PETER MATTHIESSEN

The Cloud Forest

 ECEMBER 24.
The forest increases in stature, it seems, as we ascend the river. There are fewer clearings, and the few *caboclos* standing on the bank as we go by, watching dispassion- ately as the wash from our wake bangs their frail canoes together, look darker to me, more Indian—though even a century ago, in Bates's time, the tribes of the main river banks were already extinct or absorbed by the whites

Peter Matthiessen, one of the original founders of The Paris Review, *is the author of numerous ecologically sensitive travel books and novels, such as* Far Tortuga, At Play in the Fields of the Lord, *and* The Snow Leopard, *for which he won the National Book Award in 1977. This most unusual Christmas story is from his 1961 book,* The Cloud Forest.

and Negroes. New birds continue to appear, including tropic kingfishers, one of them dark and tiny, with a white nape. In the river the floating debris is increasing, littering great areas of the expanse, but it is the jungle which changes most. A number of trees I have not noticed before, and especially one with a smooth purple-mahogany trunk—I'm told this is the purpleheart. The larger trees have aerial gardens of red-flowered epiphytes, *Bromelia*, and strange silver cylinders—these are hornets' nests—hanging like Christmas ornaments; everywhere, fastened leechlike to the trunks, are the dark masses of white ants' nests. The lowest branches of these trees must be fifty feet from the ground; in the evening light, its pale marble columns mysterious in the greens, the forest is truly beautiful; it is difficult to conceive of a lovelier forest in the world.

Tonight is Christmas Eve.

CHRISTMAS DAY.
Early on Christmas morning two brilliant macaws streamed out across the river in front of the ship, and in the fiery green of the dawn bank I saw an enormous white flower. I have not seen this flower before.

We are not a religious ship, and, the Dutch missionaries having been left behind in Manaus, there was no formal worship. To soothe our savage breasts the captain played us carols on his phonograph, and a great variety of secular music as well, everything from cha-cha-cha to *The Merry Widow.* The music was absorbed attentively by a gathering of *caboclos* who convened on the bank and in their small canoes at the point near the mouth of the Urucu River where, toward noon, the ship dropped anchor in order that all her company might celebrate Christmas dinner together.

The small salon, decorated by the captain himself, was festive in a heartbreaking sort of way, and there was even a small spruce tree, a renegade from the consignment of Christmas trees left at Saint Vincent. The odor of this humble evergreen, so crisp and strange in the damp, redolent atmosphere of the jungle river, brought me as close as I have come to homesickness—I caught myself easing up to it every little while and furtively inhaling. Past the branches of the spruce, through the bright porthole, could be seen the rapt faces of the halfbreeds on the steaming bank, and the tumbled mass of the jungle rising like a great engulfing wave behind them.

The captain served rum to his passengers and officers in person (this is the custom, and later the officers would serve Christmas dinner to the stewards). He did his courtly best to make a party of it, and to my faint surprise succeeded, pouring our drinks lavishly and with grace. Emboldened by rum, and carried on at table by wine and port, we were able to don our paper hats and snap our snappers with some gusto. The chief engineer claimed the port bottle was his own, and when this claim was contested pointed at the lettering, crying out, "Me bloody name's Fernandez, isn't it?"; behind his head our young Ortega, the swiftest waiter in the world, produced a mask with red nose, mustache, and owlish glasses, and, crossing himself, clapped it suddenly on his own face.

We feasted on ham and turkey of a kind, and there were grapes and nuts in place of the usual dessert "sweet," a tapioca or semolina decked out, according to the joint daily inspiration of the cook and steward, in a variety of brilliant colors and exotic names, and resembling nothing so much, under the effects of the ship's vibration, as a low marine organism, a community of hydroid animals, shuddering with life. This staple item was suppressed upon the Lord's Day, but I have no doubt that naked masses of it, as yet unadorned, are cached somewhere about the ship, quaking away until tomorrow.

The rest of Christmas remains a little hazy in my mind. The noon euphoria was followed, by those officers not on watch, by a humid afternoon of drinking and an access of somber homesickness. Even the chief, who earlier had appropriated the comic mask and kept popping up at portholes all over the ship, now complained bitterly that the company had not sent the ship a Christmas cable. "First ship I was ever on," he grumped, "where they

didn't have the courtesy to send the lads a little message."
The third mate was snarling and unhappy, and the
Second Engineer subsequently succumbed to the eulo-
gies of Scotland, and the good life in the Far East as a
tanker "mon," for which he has become notorious on the
Venimos. (In Haiti one afternoon, forgetting where he was,
he abused the longshoremen in Chinese, and a week
later, happening upon one of the only two Chinese in
Barbados, he celebrated and "went adrift," as these men
say—he failed, that is, to appear aboard ship when his
watch came around the following day—and this for the
first time in twelve years at sea.) Unlike the Brazilian and
Peruvian crewmen, who see their families on every run,
the majority of the officers have not been at home in
months and, in a few cases, years; though the morale of
the ship is ordinarily high, there are two officers disliked
cordially by the rest, and these resentments flowered on
Christmas Day, in company with each man's longings
and eccentricities. Nevertheless, these men are generous
and intelligent (the most intelligent are Sparks and the
Third Engineer; at least, they thrash me regularly at
chess), and on this long voyage—we are now thirty-five
days out—I have made good friends among them.

By nightfall morale had restored itself somewhat.
There was a very comic and touching collection of
absurd presents which the captain presented to me with
a speech at supper, and a fine evening of lusty singing on

the afterdeck. "The Londonderry Air" bestirred the light-less jungle, and in the reflective silence afterward the air was tightened by the squeak of bats. Overhead stars livened the whole tropic sky, sparkling outward from the mast silhouettes and crowding down on the black horizons on all sides. Some of these stars, those off to the south, never rise above our night skylines in North America. It came as a start, that realization in the silent evening that these far, endless galaxies I was seeing for the first time in my life.

FYODOR DOSTOYEVSKI

Siberia

A T AN early hour, before it was light, the drum sounded, and the under-officer whose duty it was to count the convicts wished them a happy Christmas. The prisoners answered him in an amiable tone, expressing a like wish. Akim Akimitch and many others, who had their geese and their sucking-pigs, went to the kitchen, after saying their prayers, in a

The masterpieces of Fyodor Dostoyevski would fill a large book-shelf. To name a few: Friend of the Family *(1859),* Crime and Punishment *(1866),* The Gambler *(1866),* The Idiot *(1868),* The Possessed *(1869), and* The Brothers Karamazov *(1878). Along with Tolstoy, Dostoyevski is considered the premiere Russian realist and an enormous influence on storytelling in the modern novel.*

hurried manner to see where their victuals were and how they were being cooked. Through the little windows of our barracks, half hidden by snow and ice, could be seen, flaring in the darkness, the bright fire of the two kitchens where six stoves had been lighted. In the courtyard, where it was still dark, the convicts, each with a half-pelisse round his shoulders, or perhaps fully dressed, were hurrying toward the kitchen. Some of them meanwhile—a very small number—had already visited the drink-sellers.

I went out of barracks like the others. It was beginning to get late. The stars were paling; a light, icy mist was rising from the earth, and spirals of smoke ascended in curls from the chimneys. Several convicts whom I met wished me, with affability, a happy Christmas. I thanked them and returned their wishes. Some of them had never spoken to me before. Near the kitchen a convict from the military barracks, with his sheepskin on his shoulder, came up to me. Recognising me, he called out from the middle of the courtyard, "Alexander Petrovitch!" He ran toward me. I waited for him. He was a young fellow with a round face and soft eyes, not at all communicative as a rule. He had not spoken to me since my arrival, and seemed never to have noticed me. I did not know on my side what his name was. When he came up he remained planted before me, smiling a vacuous smile, but with a happy expression.

"What do you want?" I asked, not without astonishment.

He remained standing before me, still smiling and staring, without replying.

"Why, it is Christmas Day," he muttered.

He understood that he had nothing more to say, and hastened into the kitchen.

Round the flaming stoves in the kitchen the convicts were rubbing and pushing against one another, every one watching his own property. The cooks were preparing dinner, which was to take place a little earlier than usual. No one began to eat before the time, though many wished to do so; but it was necessary to be well behaved before the others. We were waiting for the priest, and the fast proceeding Christmas would not be at an end till his arrival.

At last the priest arrived, with the cross and holy water. He prayed and chanted before the image, and then turned to the convicts, who one after the other came and kissed the cross. The priest then walked through all the barracks, sprinkling them with holy water. When he got to the kitchen he praised the bread of the convict-prison, which had a reputation in the town; the convicts at once expressed a desire to send him two loaves of new bread, still hot, which an old soldier was ordered to take to his house forthwith. Almost immediately afterwards the Major and the Commandant arrived. The Commandant was liked, and even respected; he made the tour of the barracks with the Major, wished the convicts a happy Christmas, and went into the kitchen and tasted the cabbage-soup, which was excellent that day. Each convict was entitled to nearly a pound of meat, with millet-seed, and certainly the butter had not been spared. The Major saw the Commandant to the door, and then ordered the convicts to begin dinner.

MEANWHILE IT was getting dusk. Weariness and general depression were making themselves felt through the drunkenness and general debauchery. The prisoner who an hour before was holding his sides with laughter now sobbed in a corner, exceedingly drunk: others were fighting, or wandering in a tottering manner through the barracks, pale, very pale, seeking someone to quarrel with. Petroff came up to me twice. As he had drunk very little he was calm; but until the last moment he expected something which he made sure would happen—something extraordinary, and highly diverting; although he said nothing about it this could be seen from his looks. He ran from barrack to barrack, without fatigue; but nothing happened; nothing except general intoxication, idiotic insults from drunkards, and general giddiness of heated heads. . . .

But enough of this tumultuous scene, which at last came to an end. The convicts went heavily to sleep

✳

on their camp-beds. They spoke and raged during their sleep more than on other nights. Here and there they still went on playing cards. The festival looked forward to with such impatience was over; to-morrow the daily work, the hard labour, would begin again.

BRET HARTE

How Santa Claus Came to

Simpson's Bar

IT HAD been raining in the valley of the Sacramento. The North Fork had overflowed its banks, and Rattlesnake Creek was impassable. The few boulders that had marked the summer ford at Simpson's Crossing were obliterated by a vast sheet of water stretching to the foothills. The upstage was stopped at Granger's; the last mail had been abandoned in the tules, the rider swimming for his life. "An

At nineteen, New Yorker Bret Harte packed his bags and headed to California to mine gold. Somehow, he wound up writing. Throughout the 1860s, Harte chronicled the Wild West's more colorful characters in dozens of short stories, including his now-classic "How Santa Claus Came to Simpson's Bar."

area," remarked the *Sierra Avalanche*, with pensive local pride, "as large as the State of Massachusetts is now under water."

Nor was the weather any better in the foothills. The mud lay deep on the mountain road; wagons that neither physical force nor moral objurgation could move from the evil ways into which they had fallen encumbered the track, and the way to Simpson's Bar was indicated by broken-down teams and hard swearing. And further on, cut off and inaccessible, rained upon and bedraggled, smitten by high winds and threatened by high water, Simpson's Bar, on the eve of Christmas Day, 1862, clung like a swallow's nest to the rocky entablature and splintered capitals of Table Mountain, and shook in the blast.

As night shut down on the settlement, a few lights gleamed through the mist from the windows of cabins on either side of the highway, now crossed and gullied by lawless streams and swept by marauding winds. Happily most of the population were gathered at Thompson's store, clustered around a red-hot stove, at which they silently spat in some accepted sense of social communion that perhaps rendered conversation unnecessary. Indeed, most methods of diversion had long since been exhausted on Simpson's Bar; high water had suspended the regular occupations on gulch and on river, and a consequent lack of money and whiskey had taken the zest from most illegitimate recreation. Even Mr. Hamlin was fain to leave the Bar with fifty dollars in his pocket—the only amount actually realized of the large sums won by him in the successful exercise of his arduous profession. "Ef I was asked," he remarked somewhat later—"ef I was asked to pint out a purty little village where a retired sport as didn't care for money could exercise hisself, frequent and lively, I'd say Simpson's Bar; but for a young man with a large family depending on his exertions, it don't pay." As Mr. Hamlin's family consisted mainly of female adults, this remark is quoted rather to show the breadth of his humor than the exact extent of his responsibilities.

Howbeit, the unconscious objects of this satire sat that evening in the listless apathy begotten of idleness and lack of excitement. Even the sudden splashing of hoofs before the door did not arouse them. Dick Bullen alone paused in the act of scraping out his pipe, and lifted his head, but no other one of the group indicated any interest in, or recognition of, the man who entered.

It was a figure familiar enough to the company, and known in Simpson's Bar as "The Old Man." A man of perhaps fifty years; grizzled and scant of hair, but still fresh and youthful of complexion. A face full of ready but not very powerful sympathy, with a chameleonlike aptitude for taking on the shade and color of contiguous moods and feelings. He had evidently just left some hilarious companions, and did not at first notice the gravity of the group, but clapped the shoulder of the nearest man jocularly, and threw himself into a vacant chair.

"Jest heard the best thing out, boys! Ye know Smiley, over yar—Jim Smiley—funniest man in the Bar? Well, Jim was jest telling the richest yarn about"—

"Smiley's a——fool," interrupted a gloomy voice.

"A particular——skunk," added another in sepulchral accents.

A silence followed these positive statements. The Old Man glanced quickly around the group. Then his face slowly changed. "That's so," he said reflectively, after a pause, "certainly a sort of a skunk and suthin' of a fool. In course." He was silent for a moment, as in painful contemplation of the unsavoriness and folly of the unpopular Smiley. "Dismal weather, ain't it?" he added, now fully embarked on the current of prevailing sentiment. "Mighty rough papers on the boys, and no show for money this season. And tomorrow's Christmas."

There was a movement among the men at this announcement, but whether of satisfaction or disgust was not plain. "Yes," continued the Old Man in the lugubrious tone he had within the last few moments unconsciously adopted—"yes, Christmas, and tonight's Christmas Eve. Ye see, boys, I kinder thought—that is, I sorter had an idee, jest passin' like, you know—that maybe ye'd all like to come over to my house tonight and have a sort of tear round. But I suppose, now, you wouldn't? Don't feel like it, maybe?" he added with anxious sympathy, peering into the faces of his companions.

"Well, I don't know," responded Tom Flynn with some cheerfulness. "P'r'aps we may. But how about your wife, Old Man? What does *she* say to it?"

The Old Man hesitated. His conjugal experience had not been a happy one, and the fact was known to Simpson's Bar. His first wife, a delicate, pretty little woman, had suffered keenly and secretly from the jealous suspicions of her husband, until one day he invited the whole Bar to his house to expose her infidelity. On arriving, the party found the shy, petite creature quietly engaged in her household duties, and retired abashed and discomfited. But the sensitive woman did not easily recover from the shock of this extraordinary outrage. It was with difficulty she regained her equanimity sufficiently to release her lover from the closet in which he was concealed, and escape with him. She left a boy of three years to comfort her bereaved husband. The Old Man's present wife had been his cook. She was large, loyal, and aggressive.

Before he could reply, Joe Dimmick suggested with great directness that it was the "Old Man's house," and that, invoking the Divine Power, if the case were his own, he would invite whom he pleased, even if in so doing he imperiled his salvation. The Powers of Evil, he further remarked, should contend against him vainly. All this delivered with a terseness and vigor lost in this necessary translation.

"In course. Certainly. Thet's it," said the Old Man with a sympathetic frown. "Thar's no trouble about thet. It's my own house, built every stick on it myself. Don't you be afeard o' her, boys. She *may* cut up a trifle rough—ez wimmin do—but she'll come round." Secretly the Old Man trusted to the exaltation of liquor and the power of courageous example to sustain him in such an emergency.

As yet, Dick Bullen, the oracle and leader of Simpson's Bar, had not spoken. He now took his pipe from his lips. "Old Man, how's that yer Johnny gettin' on? Seems to me he didn't look so peart last time I seed him on the bluff heavin' rocks at Chinamen. Didn't seem to take much interest in it. Thar was a gang of 'em by yar yesterday—drownded out up the river—and I kinder thought o' Johnny, and how he'd miss 'em! Maybe now, we'd be in the way ef he wus sick?"

The father, evidently touched not only by this pathetic picture of Johnny's deprivation, but by the considerate delicacy of the speaker, hastened to assure him that Johnny was better, and that a "little fun might 'liven him up." Whereupon Dick arose, shook himself, and saying, "I'm ready. Lead the way, Old Man: here goes," himself led the way with a leap, a characteristic howl, and darted out into the night. As he passed through the outer room he caught up a blazing brand from the hearth. The action was repeated by the rest of the party, closely following and elbowing each other, and before the astonished proprietor of Thompson's grocery was aware of the intention of his guests, the room was deserted.

The night was pitchy dark. In the first gust of wind their temporary torches were extinguished, and only the red brands dancing and flitting in the gloom like drunken will-o'-the-wisps indicated their whereabouts. Their way led up Pine Tree Canyon, at the head of which a broad, low, bark-thatched cabin burrowed in the mountainside. It was the home of the Old Man, and the entrance to the tunnel in which he worked when he worked at all. Here the crowd paused for a moment, out of delicate deference to their host, who came up panting in the rear.

"P'r'aps ye'd better hold on a second out yer, whilst I go in and see that things is all right," said the Old Man, with an indifference he was far from feeling. The suggestion was graciously accepted, the door opened and closed on the host, and the crowd, leaning their backs against the wall and cowering under the eaves, waited and listened.

For a few moments there was no sound but the dripping of water from the eaves and the stir and rustle of wrestling boughs above them. Then the men became uneasy, and whispered suggestion and suspicion passed from the one to the other. "Reckon she's caved in his head the first lick!" "Decoyed him inter the tunnel and barred him up, likely." "Got him down and sittin' on him." "Prob'ly biling suthin' to heave on us: stand clear the door, boys!" For just then the latch clicked, the door slowly opened, and a voice said, "Come in out o' the wet."

The voice was neither that of the Old Man nor of his wife. It was the voice of a small boy, its weak treble broken by that preternatural hoarseness which only vagabondage and the habit of premature self-assertion can give. It was the face of a small boy that looked up at theirs—a face that might have been pretty, and even refined, but that it was darkened by evil knowledge from within, and dirt and hard experience from without. He had a blanket around his shoulders, and had evidently just risen from his bed. "Come in," he repeated, "and don't make no noise. The Old Man's in there talking to mar," he continued, pointing to an adjacent room which seemed to be a kitchen, from which the Old Man's voice came in deprecating accents. "Let me be," he added querulously to Dick Bullen who had caught him up, blanket and all, and was affecting to toss him into the fire, "let go o' me, you d—d old fool, d'ye hear?"

Thus adjured, Dick Bullen lowered Johnny to the ground with a smothered laugh, while the men, entering quietly, ranged themselves around a long table

✳

of rough boards which occupied the center of the room. Johnny then gravely proceeded to a cupboard and brought out several articles, which he deposited on the table. "Thar's whiskey. And crackers. And red herons. And cheese." He took a bite of the latter on his way to the table. "And sugar." He scooped up a mouthful en route with a small and very dirty hand. "And terbacker. Thar's dried appils too on the shelf, but I don't admire 'em. Appils is swellin'. Thar," he concluded, "now wade in, and don't be afeard. I don't mind the old woman. She don't b'long to *me*. S'long."

He had stepped to the threshold of a small room, scarcely larger than a closet, partitioned off from the main apartment, and holding in its dim recess a small bed. He stood there a moment looking at the company, his bare feet peeping from the blanket, and nodded.

"Hello, Johnny! You ain't goin' to turn in again, are ye?" said Dick.

"Yes, I are," responded Johnny decidedly.

"Why, wot's up, old fellow?"

"I'm sick."

"How sick?"

"I've got a fevier. And childblains. And roomatiz," returned Johnny, and vanished within. After a moment's pause, he added in the dark, apparently from under the bedclothes—"And biles!"

There was an embarrassing silence. The men

looked at each other and at the fire. Even with the appetizing banquet before them, it seemed as if they might again fall into the despondency of Thompson's grocery, when the voice of the Old Man, incautiously lifted, came deprecatingly from the kitchen.

"Certainly! Thet's so. In course they is. A gang o' lazy, drunken loafers, and that ar Dick Bullen's the orneriest of all. Didn't hev no more *sabe* than to come round yar with sickness in the house and no provision. Thet's what I said: 'Bullen,' sez I, 'it's crazy drunk you are, or a fool,' sez I, 'to think o' such a thing.' 'Staples,' I sez, 'be you a man, Staples, and 'spect to raise h—ll under my roof and invalids lyin' round?" But they would come—they would. Thet's wot you must 'spect o' such trash as lays round the Bar."

A burst of laughter from the men followed this unfortunate exposure. Whether it was overheard in the kitchen, or whether the Old Man's irate companion had just then exhausted all other modes of expressing her contemptuous indignation, I cannot say, but a back door was suddenly slammed with great violence. A moment later and the Old Man reappeared, haply unconscious of the cause of the late hilarious outburst, and smiled blandly.

"The old woman thought she'd jest run over to Mrs. MacFadden's for a sociable call," he explained with jaunty indifference, as he took a seat on the board.

Oddly enough it needed this untoward incident to relieve the embarrassment that was beginning to be felt by the party, and their natural audacity returned with their host. I do not propose to record the convivialities of that evening. The inquisitive reader will accept the statement that the conversation was characterized by the same intellectual exaltation, the same cautious reverence, the same fastidious delicacy, the same rhetorical precision, and the same logical and coherent discourse somewhat later in the evening, which distinguish similar gatherings of the masculine sex in more civilized localities and under more favorable auspices. No glasses were broken in the absence of any; no liquor was uselessly spilt on the floor or table in the scarcity of that article.

It was nearly midnight when the festivities were interrupted. "Hush," said Dick Bullen, holding up his hand. It was the querulous voice of Johnny from his adjacent closet: "O dad!"

The Old Man arose hurriedly and disappeared in the closet. Presently he reappeared. "His rheumatiz is coming on agin bad," he explained, "and he wants rubbin'." He lifted the demijohn of whiskey from the table and shook it. It was empty. Dick Bullen put down his tin cup with an embarrassed laugh. So did the others. The Old Man examined their contents and said hopefully, "I reckon that's enough; he don't need much. You hold on all o' you for a spell, and I'll be back"; and vanished in the closet with an old flannel shirt and the whiskey. The door closed but imperfectly, and the following dialogue was distinctly audible:

"Now, sonny, whar does she ache worst?"

"Sometimes over yar and sometimes under yer; but it's most powerful from yer to yer. Rub yer, dad."

A silence seemed to indicate a brisk rubbing. Then Johnny:

"Hevin' a good time out yer, dad?"

"Yes, sonny."

"Tomorrer's Chrismiss—ain't it?"

"Yes, sonny. How does she feel now?"

"Better. Rub a little furder down. Wot's Chrismiss, anyway? Wot's it all about?"

"Oh, it's a day."

This exhaustive definition was apparently satisfactory, for there was a silent interval of rubbing. Presently Johnny again:

"Mar sez that everywhere else but yer everybody gives things to everybody Chrismiss, and then she jist waded inter you. She sez thar's a man they call Sandy Claws, not a white man, you know, but a kind o' Chinemin, comes down the chimbley night afore Chrismiss and gives things to chillern—boys like me. Puts 'em in their butes! Thet's what she tried to play upon me. Easy now, pop, whar are you rubbin' to—thet's a mile from the place. She jest made that up, didn't she, jest to aggrewate me and you? Don't rub thar. . . . Why, dad!"

In the great quiet that seemed to have fallen upon the house the sigh of the near pines and the drip of leaves without was very distinct. Johnny's voice, too, was lowered as he went on, "Don't you take on now, for I'm gettin' all right fast. Wot's the boys doin' out thar?"

The Old Man partly opened the door and peered through. His guests were sitting there sociably enough, and there were a few silver coins and a lean buckskin purse on the table. "Bettin' on suthin'—some little game or 'nother. They're all right," he replied to Johnny, and recommended his rubbing.

"I'd like to take a hand and win some money," said Johnny reflectively after a pause.

The Old Man glibly repeated what was evidently a familiar formula, that if Johnny would wait until he struck it rich in the tunnel he'd have lots of money, etc, etc.

"Yes," said Johnny, "but you don't. And whether you strike it or I win it, it's about the same. It's all luck. But it's mighty cur'o's about Chrismiss—ain't it? Why do they call it Chrismiss?"

Perhaps from some instinctive deference to the overhearing of his guests, or from some vague sense of incongruity, the Old Man's reply was so low as to be inaudible beyond the room.

"Yes," said Johnny, with some slight abatement of

interest, "I've heard o' *him* before. Thar, that'll do, dad. I don't ache near so bad as I did. Now wrap me tight in this yer blanket. So. Now," he added in a muffled whisper, "sit down yer by me till I go asleep." To assure himself of obedience, he disengaged one hand from the blanket, and grasping his father's sleeve, again composed himself to rest.

For some moments the Old Man waited patiently. Then the unwonted stillness of the house excited his curiosity, and without moving from the bed he cautiously opened the door with his disengaged hand, and looked into the main room. To his infinite surprise it was dark and deserted. But even then a smoldering log on the hearth broke, and by the upspringing blaze he saw the figure of Dick Bullen sitting by the dying embers.

"Hello!"

Dick started, rose, and came somewhat unsteadily toward him.

"Whar's the boys?" said the Old Man.

"Gone up the canyon on a little *pasear*. They're coming back for me in a minit. I'm waitin' round for 'em. What are you starin' at, Old Man?" he added, with a forced laugh; "do you think I'm drunk?"

The Old Man might have been pardoned the supposition, for Dick's eyes were humid and his face flushed. He loitered and lounged back to the chimney, yawned, shook himself, buttoned up his coat, and laughed. "Liquor ain't so plenty as that, Old Man. Now don't you get up," he continued, as the Old Man made a movement to release his sleeve from Johnny's hand. "Don't you mind manners. Sit jest whar you be; I'm goin' in a jiffy. Thar, that's them now."

There was a low tap at the door. Dick Bullen opened it quickly, nodded "good night" to his host, and disappeared. The Old Man would have followed him but for the hand that still unconsciously grasped his sleeve. He could have easily disengaged it: it was small, weak, and emaciated. But perhaps because it *was* small, weak, and emaciated he changed his mind, and drawing his chair closer to the bed, rested his head upon it. In this defenseless attitude the potency of his earlier potations surprised him. The room flickered and faded before his eyes, reappeared, faded again, went out, and left him—asleep.

Meantime Dick Bullen, closing the door, confronted his companions. "Are you ready?" said Staples. "Ready," said Dick; "what's the time?" "Past twelve," was the reply; "can you make it?—it's nigh on fifty miles, the round trip hither and yon." "I reckon," returned Dick shortly. "Whar's the mare?" "Bill and Jack's holdin' her at the crossin'." "Let 'em hold on a minit longer," said Dick.

He turned and re-entered the house softly. By the light of the guttering candle and dying fire he saw that the door of the little room was open. He stepped toward it on tiptoe and looked in. The Old Man had fallen back in his chair, snoring, his helpless feet thrust out in a line with his collapsed shoulders, and his hat pulled over his eyes. Beside him, on a narrow wooden bedstead, lay Johnny, muffled tightly in a blanket that hid all save a strip of forehead and a few curls damp with perspiration. Dick Bullen made a step forward, hesitated, and glanced over his shoulder into the deserted room. Everything was quiet. With a sudden resolution he parted his huge mustaches with both hands and stooped over the sleeping boy. But even as he did so a mischievous blast, lying in wait, swooped down the chimney, rekindled the hearth, and lit up the room with a shameless glow from which Dick fled in bashful terror.

His companions were already waiting for him at the crossing. Two of them were struggling in the darkness with some strange misshapen bulk, which as Dick came nearer took the semblance of a great yellow horse.

It was the mare. She was not a pretty picture. From her Roman nose to her rising haunches, from her arched spine hidden by the stiff *machillas* of a Mexican saddle, to her thick, straight bony legs, there was not a line of equine grace. In her half-blind but wholly vicious white eyes, in her protruding underlip, in her monstrous color, there was nothing but ugliness and vice.

"Now then," said Staples, "stand cl'ar of her heels, boys, and up with you. Don't miss your first holt of her

✳

mane, and mind ye get your off stirrup *quick*. Ready!"

There was a leap, a scrambling struggle, a bound, a wild retreat of the crowd, a circle of flying hoofs, two springless leaps that jarred the earth, a rapid play and jingle of spurs, a plunge, and then the voice of Dick somewhere in the darkness. "All right!"

"Don't take the lower road back onless you're hard pushed for time! Don't hold her in downhill! We'll be at the ford at five. G'lang! Hoopa! Mula! GO!"

A splash, a spark struck from the ledge in the road, a clatter in the rocky cut beyond, and Dick was gone.

SING, O Muse, the ride of Richard Bullen! Sing, O Muse, of chivalrous men! the sacred quest, the doughty deeds, the battery of low churls, the fearsome ride and gruesome perils of the Flower of Simpson's Bar! Alack! she is dainty, this Muse! She will have none of this bucking brute and swaggering, ragged rider, and I must fain follow him in prose, afoot!

It was one o'clock, and yet he had only gained Rattlesnake Hill. For in that time Jovita had rehearsed to him all her imperfections and practiced all her vices. Thrice had she stumbled. Twice had she thrown up her Roman nose in a straight line with the reins, and resisting bit and spur, struck out madly across country. Twice had she reared, and rearing, fallen backward; and twice had agile Dick, unharmed, regained his seat before she found her vicious legs again. And a mile beyond them, at the foot of a long hill, was Rattlesnake Creek. Dick knew that here was the crucial test of his ability to perform his enterprise, set his teeth grimly, put his knees well into her flanks, and changed his defensive tactics to brisk aggression. Bullied and maddened, Jovita began the descent of the hill. Here the artful Richard pretended to hold her in with ostentatious objurgation and well-feigned cries of alarm. It is unnecessary to add that Jovita instantly ran away. Nor need I state the time made in the descent; it is written in the chronicles of Simpson's Bar. Enough that in another moment, as it seemed to Dick, she was splashing on the overflowed banks of Rattlesnake Creek. As Dick expected, the momentum she had acquired carried her beyond the point of balking, and holding her well together for a mighty leap, they dashed into the middle of the swiftly flowing current. A few moments of kicking, wading, and swimming, and Dick drew a long breath on the opposite bank.

The road from Rattlesnake Creek to Red Mountain was tolerably level. Either the plunge in Rattlesnake Creek had dampened her baleful fire, or the art which led to it had shown her the superior wicked-ness of her rider, Jovita no longer wasted her surplus energy in wanton conceits. Once she bucked, but it was from force of habit; once she shied, but it was from a new,

✳

freshly painted meetinghouse at the crossing of the county road. Hollows, ditches, gravelly deposits, patches of fresh-ly springing grasses, flew from beneath her rattling hoofs. She began to smell unpleasantly, once or twice she coughed slightly, but there was no abatement of her strength or speed. By two o'clock he had passed Red Mountain and begun the descent to the plain. Ten minutes later the driver of the fast Pioneer coach was overtaken and passed by a "man on a pinto hoss"—an event suffi-ciently notable for remark. At half-past two Dick rose in his stirrups with a great shout. Stars were glittering through the rifted clouds, and beyond him, out of the plain, rose two spires, a flagstaff, and a straggling line of black objects. Dick jingled his spurs and swung his *riata*, Jovita bounded forward, and in another moment they swept into Tuttleville, and drew up before the wooden piazza of "The Hotel of All Nations."

What transpired that night at Tuttleville is not strictly a part of this record. Briefly I may state, however, that after Jovita had been handed over to a sleepy ostler, whom she at once kicked into unpleasant consciousness, Dick sallied out with the barkeeper for a tour of the sleeping town. Lights still gleamed from a few saloons and gambling houses; but avoiding these, they stopped before several closed shops, and by persistent tapping and judicious outcry roused the proprietors from their beds, and made them unbar the doors of their magazines and expose their wares. Sometimes they were met by curses, but oftener by interest and some concern in their needs, and the interview was invariably concluded by a drink. It was three o'clock before this pleasantry was given over, and with a small waterproof bag of India rubber strapped on his shoulders, Dick returned to the hotel. But here he was waylaid by Beauty—Beauty opulent in charms, affluent in dress, persuasive in speech, and Spanish in accent! In vain she repeated the invitation in "Excelsior," happily scorned by all Alpine-climbing youth, and rejected by this child of the Sierras—a rejection softened in this instance by a laugh and his last gold coin. And then he sprang to the saddle and dashed down the lonely street and out into the lonelier plain, where presently the lights, the black line of houses, the spires, and the flagstaff sank in the earth behind him again and were lost in the distance.

The storm had cleared away, the air was brisk and cold, the outlines of adjacent landmarks were distinct, but it was half-past four before Dick reached the meetinghouse and the crossing of the county road. To avoid the rising grade he had taken a longer and more circuitous road, in whose viscid mud Jovita sank fetlock deep at every bound. It was a poor preparation for a steady ascent of five miles more; but Jovita, gathering her legs under her, took it with her usual blind, unreasoning fury, and a half-hour later reached the long level that led to Rattlesnake Creek. Another half-hour would bring him to the creek. He threw the reins lightly upon the neck of the mare, chirruped to her, and began to sing.

Suddenly Jovita shied with a bound that would have unseated a less practiced rider. Hanging to her rein was a figure that had leaped from the bank, and at the same time from the road before her arose a shadowy horse and rider.

"Throw up your hands," commanded the second apparition, with an oath.

Dick felt the mare tremble, quiver, and apparently sink under him. He knew what it meant and was prepared.

"Stand aside, Jack Simpson. I know you, you d—d thief! Let me pass, or—"

He did not finish the sentence. Jovita rose straight in the air with a terrific bound, throwing the figure from her bit with a single shake of her vicious head, and charged with deadly malevolence down on the impediment before her. An oath, a pistol shot, horse and highwayman rolled over in the road, and the next moment Jovita was a hundred yards away. But the good right arm of her rider, shattered by a bullet, dropped helplessly at his side.

Without slacking his speed he shifted the reins to his left hand. But a few moments later he was obliged to halt and tighten the saddle girths that had slipped in the onset. This in his crippled condition took some time. He had no fear of pursuit, but looking up he saw that the eastern stars were already paling, and that the distant peaks had lost their ghostly whiteness and now stood out blackly against a lighter sky. Day was upon him. Then completely absorbed in a single idea, he forgot the pain of his wound, and mounting again dashed on toward Rattlesnake Creek. But now Jovita's breath came broken by gasps, Dick reeled in his saddle, and brighter and brighter grew the sky.

Ride, Richard; run, Jovita; linger, O day!

For the last few rods there was a roaring in his ears. Was it exhaustion from loss of blood, or what? He was dazed and giddy as he swept down the hill, and did not recognize his surroundings. Had he taken the wrong road, or was this Rattlesnake Creek?

It was. But the brawling creek he had swum a few hours before had risen, more than doubled its volume, and now rolled a swift and resistless river between him and Rattlesnake Hill. For the first time that night Richard's heart sank within him. The river, the mountain, the quickening east, swam before his eyes. He shut them to recover his self-control. In that brief interval, by some fantastic mental process, the little room at Simpson's Bar and the figures of the sleeping father and son rose upon him. He opened his eyes wildly, cast off his coat, pistol, boots, and saddle, bound his precious pack tightly to his shoulders, grasped the bare flanks of Jovita with his bared knees, and with a shout dashed into the yellow water. A cry rose from the opposite bank as the head of a man and horse struggled for a few moments against the battling current, and then were swept away amidst uprooted trees and whirling driftwood.

THE OLD Man started and woke. The fire on the hearth was dead, the candle in the outer room flickering in its socket, and somebody was rapping at the door. He opened it, but fell back with a cry before the dripping, half-naked figure that reeled against the doorpost.

"Dick?"

"Hush! Is he awake yet?"

"No; but, Dick—"

"Dry up, you old fool! Get me some whiskey, *quick!*" The Old Man flew and returned with—an empty bottle! Dick would have sworn, but his strength was not equal to the occasion. He staggered, caught at the handle of the door, and motioned to the Old Man.

"Thar's suthin' in my pack yer for Johnny. Take it off. I can't."

The Old Man unstrapped the pack, and laid it before the exhausted man.

"Open it, quick."

He did so with trembling fingers. It contained

only a few poor toys—cheap and barbaric enough, goodness knows, but bright with paint and tinsel. One of them
was broken; another, I fear, was irretrievably ruined by
water, and on the third—ah me! there was a cruel spot.

"It don't look like much, that's a fact," said Dick
ruefully.... "But it's the best we could do.... Take 'em, Old
Man, and put 'em in his stocking, and tell him—tell him,
you know—hold me, Old Man—" The Old Man caught at
his sinking figure. "Tell him," said Dick, with a weak little laugh—"tell him Sandy Claus has come."

And even so, bedraggled, ragged, unshaven and
unshorn, with one arm hanging helplessly at his side,
Santa Claus came to Simpson's Bar and fell fainting on
the first threshold. The Christmas dawn came slowly
after, touching the remoter peaks with the rosy warmth
of ineffable love. And it looked so tenderly on Simpson's
Bar that the whole mountain, as if caught in a generous
action, blushed to the skies.

CHARLES DICKENS

A Christmas Tree

I HAVE BEEN looking on, this evening, at a merry company of children assembled round that pretty German toy, a Christmas Tree. The tree was planted in the middle of a great round table, and towered high above their heads. It was brilliantly lighted by a multitude of little tapers; and everywhere sparkled and glittered with bright objects. There were

English novelist Charles Dickens's subject was always the same: decrepit 1800s London society and its horrible treatment of the poor. This theme runs through his major works: Oliver Twist, Bleak House, and David Copperfield. "A Christmas Tree" was written during a relatively upbeat five-year period in the 1840s, when Dickens produced a series of Christmas stories, including A Christmas Carol.

rosy-cheeked dolls, hiding behind the green leaves; and there were real watches (with movable hands, at least, and an endless capacity of being wound up) dangling from innumerable twigs; there were French-polished tables, chairs, bedsteads, wardrobes, eight-day clocks, and various other articles of domestic furniture (wonderfully made, in tin, at Wolverhampton), perched among the boughs, as if in preparation for some fairy house-keeping; there were jolly, broad-faced little men, much more agreeable in appearance than many real men—and no wonder, for their heads took off, and showed them to be full of sugar-plums; there were fiddles and drums; there were tambourines, books, work-boxes, paint-boxes, sweet-meat-boxes, peep-show boxes, and all kinds of boxes; there were trinkets for the elder girls, far brighter than any grown-up gold and jewels; there were baskets and pin-cushions in all devices; there were guns, swords, and banners; there were witches standing in enchanted rings of pasteboard, to tell fortunes; there were teetotums, humming-tops, needle-cases, pen-wipers, smelling-bottles, conversation-cards, bouquet-holders; real fruit, made artificially dazzling with gold leaf; imitation apples, pears, and walnuts, crammed with surprises; in short, as a pretty child, before me, delightedly whispered to another pretty child, her bosom friend, "There was everything, and more." This motley collection of odd objects, clustering on the tree like magic fruit, and flashing back the bright looks directed toward it from every side—some of the diamond-eyes admiring it were hardly on a level with the table, and a few were languishing in timid wonder on the bosoms of pretty mothers, aunts, and nurses—made a lively realization of the fancies of childhood; and set me thinking how all the trees that grow and all the things that come into existence on the earth, have their wild adornments at that well-remembered time.

Being now at home again, and alone, the only person in the house awake, my thoughts are drawn back, by a fascination which I do not care to resist, to my own childhood. I begin to consider, what do we all remember best upon the branches of the Christmas Tree of our own young Christmas days, by which we climbed to real life.

Straight, in the middle of the room, cramped in the freedom of its growth by no encircling walls or soon-reached ceiling, a shadowy tree arises; and, looking up into the dreamy brightness of its top—for I observe in this tree the singular property that it appears to grow downward toward the earth—I look into my youngest Christmas recollections!

All toys are first, I find. Up yonder, among the green holly and red berries, is the Tumbler with his hands in his pockets, who wouldn't lie down, but whenever he was put upon the floor, persisted in rolling his fat body about, until he rolled himself still, and brought those lobster eyes of his to bear upon me—when I affected

✳

to laugh very much, but in my heart of hearts was extremely doubtful of him. Close beside him is that infernal snuff-box, out of which sprang a demoniacal Counsellor in a black gown, with an obnoxious head of hair, and a red cloth mouth, wide open, who was not to be endured on any terms, but could not be put away either; for he used suddenly, in a highly magnified state, to fly out of Mammoth Snuff-boxes in dreams, when least expected. Nor is the frog with cobbler's wax on his tail, far off; for there was no knowing where he wouldn't jump; and when he flew over the candle, and came upon one's hand with that spotted back—red on a green ground—he was horrible. The cardboard lady in a blue-silk skirt, who was stood up against the candlestick to dance, and whom I see on the same branch, was milder, and was beautiful; but I can't say as much for the larger cardboard man, who used to be hung against the wall and pulled by a string; there was a sinister expression in that nose of his; and when he got his legs round his neck (which he very often did), he was ghastly, and not a creature to be alone with.

When did that dreadful Mask first look at me? Who put it on, and why was I so frightened that the sight of it is an era in my life? It is not a hideous visage in itself; it is even meant to be droll; why then were its stolid features so intolerable? Surely not because it hid the wearer's face. An apron would have done as much; and though I should have preferred even the apron away, it would not have been absolutely insupportable, like the mask. Was it the immovability of the mask? The doll's face was immovable, but I was not afraid of *her*. Perhaps that fixed and set change coming over a real face, infused into my quickened heart some remote suggestion and dread of the universal change that is to come on every face, and make it still? Nothing reconciled me to it. No drummers, from whom proceeded a melancholy chirping on the turning of a handle; no regiment of soldiers, with a mute band, taken out of a box, and fitted, one by one, upon a stiff and lazy little set of lazy-tongs; no old woman, made of wires and a brown-paper composition, cutting up a pie for two small children; could give me a permanent comfort, for a long time. Nor was it any satisfaction to be shown the Mask, and see that it was made of paper, or to have it locked up and be assured that no one wore it. The mere recollection of that fixed face, the mere knowledge of its existence anywhere, was sufficient to awake me in the night all perspiration and horror, with, 'O I know it's coming! O the mask!'

I never wondered what the dear old donkey with the panniers—there he is! was made of, then! His hide was real to the touch, I recollect. And the great black horse with the round red spots all over him—the horse that could even get upon—I never wondered what had brought him to that strange condition, or thought that

such a horse was not commonly seen at Newmarket. The
four horses of no colour, next to him, that went into the
waggon of cheeses, and could be taken out and stabled
under the piano, appear to have bits of fur-tippet for their
tails, and other bits for their manes, and to stand on pegs
instead of legs, but it was not so when they were brought
home for a Christmas present. They were all right, then;
neither was their harness unceremoniously nailed into
their chests, as appears to be the case now. The tinkling
works of the music-cart, I *did* find out, to be made of quill
tooth-picks and wire; and I always thought that little
tumbler in his shirt sleeves, perpetually swarming up
one side of a wooden frame, and coming down, head fore-
most, on the other, rather a weak-minded person—
though good-natured; but the Jacob's Ladder, next him,
made of little squares of red wood, that went flapping
and clattering over one another, each developing a different picture, and the whole enlivened by small bells, was a
mighty marvel and a great delight.

Ah! The Doll's house!—of which I was not proprietor, but where I visited. I don't admire the Houses of
Parliament half so much as that stone-fronted mansion
with real glass windows, and door-steps, and a real
balcony—greener than I ever see now, except at water-
ing-places; and even they afford but a poor imitation.
And though it *did* open all at once, the entire house-front
(which was a blow, I admit, as cancelling the fiction of a

staircase), it was but to shut it up again, and I could believe. Even open, there were three distinct rooms in it: a sitting-room and bed-room, elegantly furnished, and best of all, a kitchen, with uncommonly soft fire-irons, a plentiful assortment of diminutive utensils—oh, the warming-pan!—and a tin man-cook in profile, who was always going to fry two fish. What Barmecide justice have I done to the noble feasts wherein the set of wooden platters figured, each with its own peculiar delicacy, as a ham or turkey, glued tight on to it, and garnished with something green, which I recollect as moss! Could all the Temperance Societies of these later days, united, give me such a tea-drinking as I have had through the means of yonder little set of blue crockery, which really would hold liquid (it ran out of the small wooden cask, I recollect, and tasted of matches), and which made tea, nectar. And if the two legs of the ineffectual little sugar-tongs did tumble over one another, and want purpose, like Punch's hands, what does it matter? And if I did once shriek out, as a poisoned child, and strike the fashionable company with consternation, by reason of having drunk a little teaspoon, inadvertently dissolved in too hot tea, I was never the worse for it, except by a powder!

Upon the next branches of the tree, lower down, hard by the green roller and miniature gardening-tools, how thick the books begin to hang. Thin books, in themselves, at first, but many of them, and with deliciously

＊

smooth covers of bright red or green. What fat black letters to begin with!"A was an archer, and shot at a frog." Of
course he was. He was an apple-pie also, and there he is!
He was a good many things in his time, was A, and so
were most of his friends, except X, who had so little ver-
satility, that I never knew him to get beyond Xerxes or
Xantippe—like Y, who was always confined to a Yacht or
a Yew Tree; and Z condemned for ever to be a Zebra or a
Zany. But, now, the very tree itself changes, and becomes
a bean-stalk—the marvellous bean-stalk up which Jack
climbed to the Giant's house! And now, those dreadfully
interesting, double-headed giants, with their clubs over
their shoulders, begin to stride along the boughs in a perfect throng, dragging knights and ladies home for dinner
by the hair of their heads. And Jack—how noble, with
his sword of sharpness, and his shoes of swiftness! Again
those old meditations come upon me as I gaze up at him;
and I debate within myself whether there was more than
one Jack (which I am loth to believe possible), or only one
genuine original admirable Jack, who achieved all the
recorded exploits.

Good for Christmas time is the ruddy color of the
cloak, in which—the tree making a forest of itself for her
to trip through, with her basket—Little Red Riding-Hood
comes to me one Christmas Eve to give me information
of the cruelty and treachery of that dissembling Wolf
who ate her grandmother, without making any

impression on his appetite, and then ate her, after making that ferocious joke about his teeth. She was my first love. I felt that if I could have married Little Red Riding-Hood, I should have known perfect bliss. But, it was not to be; and there was nothing for it but to look out the Wolf in the Noah's Ark there, and put him late in the procession on the table, as a monster who was to be degraded. O the wonderful Noah's Ark! It was not found seaworthy when put in a washing-tub, and the animals were crammed in at the roof, and needed to have their legs well shaken down before they could be got in, even there—and then, ten to one but they began to tumble out at the door, which was but imperfectly fastened with a wire latch—but what was *that* against it! Consider the noble fly, a size or two smaller than the elephant: the lady-bird, the butterfly—all triumphs of art! Consider the goose, whose feet were so small, and whose balance was so indifferent, that he usually tumbled forward, and knocked down all the animal creation. Consider Noah and his family, like idiotic tobacco-stoppers; and how the leopard stuck to warm little fingers; and now the tails of the larger animals used gradually to resolve themselves into frayed bits of string!

Hush! Again a forest, and somebody up in a tree—not Robin Hood, not Valentine, not the Yellow Dwarf (I have passed him and all Mother Bunch's wonders, without mention), but an Eastern King with a

glittering scimitar and turban. By Allah! two Eastern
Kings, for I see another, looking over his shoulder! Down
upon the grass, at the tree's foot, lies the full length of a
coal-black Giant, stretched asleep, with his head in a
lady's lap; and near them is a glass box, fastened with
four locks of shining steel, in which he keeps the lady
prisoner when he is awake. I see the four keys at his girdle now. The lady makes signs to the two kings in the
tree, who softly descend. It is the setting-in of the bright
Arabian Nights.

Oh, now all common things become uncommon
and enchanted to me. All lamps are wonderful; all rings
are talismans. Common flower-pots are full of treasure,
with a little earth scattered on the top; trees are for Ali
Baba to hide in; beef-steaks are to throw down in the
Valley of Diamonds, that the precious stones may stick to
them, and be carried by the eagles to their nests, whence
the traders, with loud cries, will scare them. Tarts are
made, according to the recipe of the Vizier's son of
Bussorah, who turned pastry-cook after he was set down
in his drawers at the gate of Damascus; cobblers are all
Mustaphas, and in the habit of sewing up people cut into
four pieces, to whom they are taken blindfold.

Any iron ring let into stone is the entrance to a
cave which only waits for the magician, and the little
fire, and the necromancy, that will make the earth shake.
All the dates imported come from the same tree as that

unlucky date, with whose shell the merchant knocked out the eye of the genie's invisible son. All olives are of the stock of that fresh fruit, concerning which the Commander of the Faithful overheard the boy conduct the fictitious trial of the fraudulent olive merchant; all apples are akin to the apple purchased (with two others) from the Sultan's gardener for three sequins, and which the tall black slave stole from the child. All dogs are associated with the dog, really a transformed man, who jumped upon the baker's counter, and put his paw on the piece of bad money. All rice recalls the rice which the awful lady, who was a ghoule, could only peck by grains, because of her nightly feasts in the burial-place. My very rocking-horse,—there he is, with his nostrils turned completely inside-out, indicative of Blood!—should have a peg in his neck, by virtue thereof to fly away with me, as the wooden horse did with the Prince of Persia, in the sight of all his father's Court.

Yes, on every object that I recognize among those upper branches of my Christmas Tree, I see this fairy light! When I wake in bed, at daybreak, on the cold dark winter mornings, the white snow dimly beheld, outside, through the frost on the window-pane, I hear Dinarzade. "Sister, sister, if you are yet awake, I pray you finish the history of the Young King of the Black Islands." Scheherazade replies, "If my lord the Sultan will suffer me to live another day, sister, I will not only finish that,

❋

but tell you a more wonderful story yet." Then, the gracious Sultan goes out, giving no orders for the execution, and we all three breathe again.

At this height of my tree I begin to see, cowering among the leaves—it may be born of turkey, or of pudding, or mince pie, or of these many fancies, jumbled with Robinson Crusoe on his desert island, Philip Quarll among the monkeys, Sandford and Merton with Mr. Barlow, Mother Bunch, and the Mask—or it may be the result of indigestion, assisted by imagination and over-doctoring—a prodigious nightmare. It is so exceedingly indistinct, that I don't know why it's frightful—but I know it is. I can only make out that it is an immense array of shapeless things, which appear to be planted on a vast exaggeration of the lazy-tongs that used to bear the toy soldiers, and to be slowly coming close to my eyes, and receding to an immeasurable distance. When it comes closest, it is worst. In connection with it I descry remembrances of winter nights incredibly long; of being sent early to bed, as a punishment for some small offence, and waking in two hours, with a sensation of having been asleep two nights; of the laden hopelessness of morning ever dawning; and the oppression of a weight of remorse.

And now, I see a wonderful row of little lights rise smoothly out of the ground, before a vast green curtain. Now, a bell rings—a magic bell, which still sounds in my ears unlike all other bells—and music plays, amidst a

buzz of voices, and a fragrant smell of orange-peel and oil.
Anon, the magic bell commands the music to cease, and
the great green curtain rolls itself up majestically, and
The Play begins! The devoted dog of Montargis avenges
the death of his master, foully murdered in the Forest of
Bondy; and a humorous Peasant with a red nose and a
very little hat, whom I take from this hour forth to my
bosom as a friend (I think he was a Waiter or an Hostler
at a village Inn, but many years have passed since he and
I have met), remarks that the sassigassity of that dog is
indeed surprising; and evermore this jocular conceit will
live in my remembrance fresh and unfading, overtop-
ping all possible jokes, unto the end of time. Or now, I
learn with bitter tears how poor Jane Shore, dressed all in
white, and with her brown hair hanging down, went
starving through the streets; or how George Barnwell
killed the worthiest uncle that ever man had, and was
afterward so sorry for it that he ought to have been let off.
Comes swift to comfort me, the Pantomime—stupendous
Phenomenon!—when clowns are shot from loaded mor-
tars into the great chandelier, bright constellation that it
is; when Harlequins, covered all over with scales of pure
gold, twist and sparkle, like amazing fish; when
Pantaloon (whom I deem it no irreverence to compare in
my own mind to my grandfather) puts red-hot pokers in
his pocket, and cries "Here's somebody coming!" or taxes
the Clown with petty larceny, by saying, "Now, I sawed

you do it!" when Everything is capable, with the greatest ease, of being changed into Anything; and "Nothing is, but thinking makes it so." Now, too, I perceive my first experience of the dreary sensation—often to return in after-life—of being unable, next day, to get back to the dull, settled world; of wanting to live for ever in the bright atmosphere I have quitted; of doting on the little Fairy, with the wand like a celestial Barber's Pole, and pining for a Fairy immortality along with her. Ah, she comes back, in many shapes, as my eye wanders down the branches of my Christmas Tree, and goes as often, and has never yet stayed by me!

Out of this delight springs the toy-theatre—there it is, with its familiar proscenium, and ladies in feathers, in the boxes!—and all its attendant occupation with paste and glue, and gum, and water colors, in the getting-up of The Miller and his Men, and Elizabeth, or the Exile of Siberia. In spite of a few besetting accidents and failures (particularly an unreasonable disposition in the respectable Kelmar, and some others, to become faint in the legs, and double up, at exciting points of the drama), a teeming world of fancies so suggestive and all-embracing, that, far below it on my Christmas Tree, I see dark, dirty, real Theaters in the day-time, adorned with these associations as with the freshest garlands of the rarest flowers, and charming me yet.

But hark! The Waits are playing, and they break

my childish sleep! What images do I associate with the
Christmas music as I see them set forth on the Christmas
Tree? Known before all the others, keeping far apart from
all the others, they gather round my little bed. An angel,
speaking to a group of shepherds in a field; some trav-
ellers, with eyes uplifted, following a star; a baby in a
manger; a child in a spacious temple, talking with grave
men; a solemn figure, with a mild and beautiful face, rais-
ing a dead girl by the hand; again, near a city gate, calling
back the son of a widow, on his bier, to life; a crowd of
people looking through the opened roof of a chamber
where he sits, and letting down a sick person on a bed,
with ropes; the same, in a tempest, walking on the water
to a ship; again, on a sea-shore, teaching a great multitude;
again, with a child upon his knee, and other children
round; again, restoring sight to the blind, speech to the
dumb, hearing to the deaf, health to the sick, strength to
the lame, knowledge to the ignorant; again, dying upon a
Cross, watched by armed soldiers, a thick darkness coming on, the earth beginning to shake, and only one voice
heard, "Forgive them, for they know not what they do."

Still, on the lower and maturer branches of the
Tree, Christmas associations cluster thick. School-books
shut up; Ovid and Virgil silenced; the Rule of Three,
with its cool impertinent inquiries, long disposed of;
Terence and Plautus acted no more, in an arena of hud-
dled desks and forms, all chipped, and notched, and

✳

inked; cricket-bars, stumps, and balls, left higher up, with
the smell of trodden grass and the softened noise of
shouts in the evening air; the tree is still fresh, still gay. If I
no more come home at Christmas time, there will be
boys and girls (thank Heaven!) while the World lasts;
and they do! Yonder they dance and play upon the
branches of my Tree, God bless them, merrily, and my
heart dances and plays too!

And I *do* come home at Christmas. We all do, or
we all should. We all come home, or ought to come home,
for a short holiday—the longer, the better—from the great
boarding-school, where we are for ever working at our
arithmetical slates, to take, and give a rest. As to going a
visiting, where can we not go, if we will; where have we
not been, when we would; starting our fancy from our
Christmas Tree!

Away into the winter prospect. There are many
such upon the tree! On, by low-lying, misty grounds,
through fens and fogs, up long hills, winding dark as cav-
erns between thick plantations, almost shutting out the
sparkling stars; so, out on broad heights, until we stop at
last, with sudden silence, at an avenue. The gate-bell has a
deep, half-awful sound in the frosty air; the gate swings
open on its hinges; and, as we drive up to a great house,
the glancing lights grow larger in the windows, and the
opposing rows of trees seem to fall solemnly back on
either side, to give us place. At intervals, all day, a fright-

ened hare has shot across this whitened turf, or the distant clatter of a herd of deer trampling the hard frost, has,
for the minute, crushed the silence too. Their watchful
eyes beneath the fern may be shining now, if we could
see them, like the icy dewdrops on the leaves; but they
are still, and all is still. And so, the lights growing larger,
and the trees falling back before us, and closing up again
behind us, as if to forbid retreat, we come to the house.

There is probably a smell of roasted chestnuts
and other good comfortable things all the time, for we are
telling Winter Stories—Ghost Stories, or more shame for
us—round the Christmas fire; and we have never stirred,
except to draw a little nearer to it. But, no matter for that.
We came to the house, and it is an old house, full of great
chimneys where wood is burnt on ancient dogs upon
the hearth, and grim portraits (some of them with grim
legends, too) lower distrustfully from the oaken panels of
the walls. We are a middle-aged nobleman, and we make
a generous supper with our host and hostess and their
guests—it being Christmas-time, and the old house full of
company—and then we go to bed. Our room is a very old
room. It is hung with tapestry. We don't like the portrait
of a cavalier in green, over the fireplace. There are great
black beams in the ceiling, and there is a great black bedstead, supported at the foot by two great black figures,
who seem to have come off a couple of tombs in the old
baronial church in the park, for our particular accommo-

dation. But, we are not a superstitious nobleman, and we don't mind. Well! we dismiss our servant, lock to the door, and sit before the fire in our dressing-gown, musing about a great many things. At length we go to bed. Well! we can't sleep. We toss and tumble, and can't sleep. The embers on the hearth burn fitfully and make the room look ghostly. We can't help peeping out over the counter-pane, at the two black figures and the cavalier—that wicked-looking cavalier—in green. In the flickering light they seem to advance and retire: which, though we are not by any means a superstitious nobleman, is not agree-able. Well! we get nervous—more and more nervous. We say "This is very foolish, but we can't stand this; we'll pretend to be ill, and knock up somebody." Well! we are just going to do it, when the locked door opens, and there comes in a young woman, deadly pale, and with long fair hair, who glides to the fire, and sits down in the chair we have left there, wringing her hands. Then, we notice that her clothes are wet. Our tongue cleaves to the roof of our mouth, and we can't speak; but, we observe her accurately. Her clothes are wet; her long hair is dabbled with moist mud; she is dressed in the fashion of two hundred years ago; and she has at her girdle a bunch of rusty keys. Well! there she sits, and we can't even faint we are in such a state about it. Presently she gets up, and tries all the locks in the room with the rusty keys, which won't fit one of them; then, she fixes her eyes on the portrait of the cavalier in green, and says, in a low, terrible voice, "The stags know it!" After that, she wrings her hands again, passes the bedside, and goes out at the door. We hurry on our dressing-gown, seize our pistols (we always travel with pistols), and are following, when we find the door locked. We turn the key, look out into the dark gallery; no one there. We wander away, and try to find our servant. Can't be done. We pace the gallery till daybreak; then return to our deserted room, fall asleep, and are awakened by our servant (nothing ever haunts *him*) and the shining sun. Well! we make a wretched breakfast, and all the company say we look queer. After breakfast, we go over the house with our host, and then we take him to the portrait of the cavalier in green, and then it all comes out. He was false to a young housekeeper once attached to that family, and famous for her beauty, who drowned herself in a pond, and whose body was discovered, after a long time, because the stags refused to drink of the water. Since which, it has been whispered that she traverses the house at midnight (but goes especially to that room where the cavalier in green was wont to sleep) trying the old locks with the rusty keys. Well! we tell our host of what we have seen, and a shade comes over his features, and he begs it may be hushed up; and so it is. But, it's all true; and we said so, before we died (we are dead now) to many responsible people.

There is no end to the old houses, with resound-

✳

ing galleries, and dismal state-bedchambers, and haunted
wings shut up for many years, through which we may
ramble, with an agreeable creeping up our back, and
encounter any number of ghosts, but (it is worthy of
remark perhaps) reducible to a very few general types
and classes; for, ghosts have little originality, and 'walk' in
a beaten track. Thus, it comes to pass, that a certain room
in a certain old hall, where a certain bad lord, baronet,
knight, or gentleman, shot himself, has certain planks in
the floor from which the blood *will* *not* be taken out. You
may scrape and scrape, as the present owner has done, or
plane and plane, as his father did, or scrub and scrub, as
his grandfather did, or burn and burn with strong acids,
as his great-grandfather did, but, there the blood will still
be—no redder and no paler—no more and no less—
always just the same. Thus, in such another house there is
a haunted door, that never will keep open; or another
door that never will keep shut; or a haunted sound of a
spinning-wheel, or a hammer, or a footstep, or a cry, or a
sigh, or a horse's tramp, or the rattling of a chain. Or else,
there is a turret-clock, which, at the midnight hour,
strikes thirteen when the head of the family is going to
die; or a shadowy, immovable black carriage which at
such a time is always seen by somebody, waiting near
the great gates in the stable-yard. Or thus, it came to pass
how Lady Mary went to pay a visit at a large wild house
in the Scottish Highlands, and, being fatigued with her

long journey, retired to bed early, and innocently said, next morning, at the breakfast-table, "How odd, to have so late a party last night, in this remote place, and not to tell me of it, before I went to bed!" Then, everyone asked Lady Mary what she meant? Then, Lady Mary replied, "Why, all night long, the carriages were driving round and round the terrace, underneath my window!" Then, the owner of the house turned pale, and so did his Lady, and Charles Macdoodle of Macdoodle signed to Lady Mary to say no more, and every one was silent. After breakfast, Charles Macdoodle told Lady Mary that it was a tradition in the family that those rumbling carriages on the terrace betokened death. And so it proved, for, two months afterward, the Lady of the mansion died. And Lady Mary, who was a Maid of Honour at Court, often told this story to the old Queen Charlotte; by this token that the old King always said, "Eh, eh? What, what? Ghosts, ghosts? No such thing, no such thing!" And never left off saying so, until he went to bed.

Or, a friend of somebody's whom most of us know, when he was a young man at college, had a particular friend, with whom he made the compact that, if it were possible for the Spirit to return to this earth after its separation from the body, he of the twin who first died, should reappear to the other. In course of time, this compact was forgotten by our friend; the two young men having progressed in life, and taken diverging paths that were wider asunder. But, one night, many years afterward, our friend being in the North of England, and staying for the night in an inn, on the Yorkshire Moors, happened to look out of bed; and there, in the moonlight, leaning on a bureau near the window, stedfastly regarding him, saw his old college friend! The appearance being solemnly addressed, replied, in a kind of whisper, but very audibly, "Do not come near me. I am dead. I am here to redeem my promise. I come from another world, but may not disclose its secrets!" Then, the whole form becoming paler, melted, as it were, into the moonlight, and faded away.

Or, there was the daughter of the first occupier of the picturesque Elizabethan house, so famous in our neighborhood. You have heard about her? No! Why, *She* went out one summer evening at twilight, when she was a beautiful girl, just seventeen years of age, to gather flowers in the garden; and presently came running, terrified, into the hall to her father, saying, "Oh, dear father, I have met myself!" He took her in his arms, and told her it was fancy, but she said, "Oh no! I met myself in the broad walk, and I was pale and gathering withered flowers, and I turned my head, and held them up!" And, that night, she died; and a picture of her story was begun, though never finished, and they say it is somewhere in the house to this day, with its face to the wall.

Or, the uncle of my brother's wife was riding

home on horseback, one mellow evening at sunset, when, in a green lane close to his own house, he saw a man standing before him, in the very centre of the narrow way. "Why does that man in the cloak stand there!" he thought. "Does he want me to ride over him?" But the figure never moved. He felt a strange sensation at seeing it so still, but slackened his trot and rode forward. When he was so close to it, as almost to touch it with his stirrup, his horse shied, and the figure glided up the bank, in a curious, unearthly manner—backward, and without seeming to use its feet—and was gone. The uncle of my brother's wife, exclaiming, "Good Heaven! It's my cousin Harry, from Bombay!" put spurs to his horse, which was suddenly in a profuse sweat, and, wondering at such a strange behaviour, dashed round to the front of his house. There, he saw the same figure, just passing in at the long French window of the drawing-room, opening on the ground. He threw his bridle to a servant, and hastened in after it. His sister was sitting there, alone. "Alice, where's my cousin Harry?" "Your cousin Harry, John?" "Yes. From Bombay. I met him in the lane just now, and saw him enter here, this instant." Not a creature had been seen by any one; and in that hour and minute, as it afterward appeared, this cousin died in India.

Or, it was a certain sensible old maiden lady, who died at ninety-nine, and retained her faculties to the last, who really did see the Orphan Boy; a story which has often been incorrectly told, but, of which the real truth is this—because it is, in fact, a story belonging to our family—and she was a connexion of our family. When she was about forty years of age, and still an uncommonly fine woman (her lover died young, which was the reason why she never married, though she had many offers), she went to stay at a place in Kent, which her brother, an Indian-Merchant, had newly bought. There was a story that this place had once been in trust, by the guardian of a young boy; who was himself the next heir, and who killed the young boy by harsh and cruel treatment. She knew nothing of that. It has been said that there was a Cage in her bedroom in which the guardian used to put the boy. There was no such thing. There was only a closet. She went to bed, made no alarm whatever in the night, and in the morning said composedly to her maid when she came in, "Who is the pretty forlorn-looking child who has been peeping out of that closet all night?" The maid replied by giving a loud scream, and instantly decamping. She was surprised; but she was a woman of remarkable strength of mind, and she dressed herself and went down stairs, and closeted herself with her brother. "Now, Walter," she said, "I have been disturbed all night by a pretty, forlorn-looking boy, who has been constantly peeping out of that closet in my room, which I can't open. This is some trick." "I am afraid not, Charlotte," said he, "for it is the legend of the house. It is the Orphan Boy. What did he do?" "He opened the door softly" said she, "and peeped out. Sometimes, he came a step or two into the room. Then, I called to him, to encourage him, and he shrunk, and shuddered, and crept in again, and shut the door." "The closet has no communication, Charlotte," said her brother, "with any other part of the house, and it's nailed up." This was undeniably true, and it took two carpenters a whole forenoon to get it open, for examination. Then, she was satisfied that she had seen the Orphan Boy. But, the wild and terrible part of the story is, that he was also seen by three of her brother's sons, in succession, who all died young. On the occasion of each child being taken ill, he came home in a heat, twelve hours before, and said, Oh, Mamma, he had been playing under a particular oak-tree, in a certain meadow, with a strange boy—a pretty, forlorn-looking boy, who was very timid, and made signs! From fatal experience, the parents came to know that this was the Orphan Boy, and that the course of that child whom he chose for his little playmate was surely run.

Legion is the name of the German castles, where we sit up alone to wait for the Spectre—where we are shown into a room, made comparatively cheerful for our reception—where we glance round at the shadows, thrown on the blank walls by the crackling fire—where we feel very lonely when the village innkeeper and his pretty daughter have retired, after laying down a fresh stone of wood upon the hearth, and setting forth on the small table such supper-cheer as a cold roast capon, bread, grapes, and a flask of old Rhine wine—where the reverberating doors close on their retreat, one after another, like so many peals of sullen thunder—and where, about the small hours of the night, we come into the knowledge of diverse supernatural mysteries. Legion is the name of the haunted German students, in whose society we draw yet nearer to the fire, while the schoolboy in the corner opens his eyes wide and round, and flies off the footstool he has chosen for his seat, when the door accidentally blows open. Vast is the crop of such fruit, shining on our Christmas Tree; in blossom, almost at the very top; ripening all down the boughs!

Among the later toys and fancies hanging there—as idle often and less pure—be the images once associated with the sweet old Waits, the softened music in the night, ever unalterable! Encircled by the social thoughts of Christmas time, still let the benignant figure of my childhood stand unchanged! In every cheerful image and suggestion that the season brings, may the bright star that rested above the poor roof, be the star of all the Christian World! A moment's pause, O vanishing tree, of which the lower boughs are dark to me as yet, and let me look once more! I know there are blank spaces on thy branches, where eyes that I have loved, have shone and smiled; from which they are departed. But, far above,

✳

I see the raiser of the dead girl, and the Widow's Son; and God is good! If Age be hiding for me in the unseen portion of thy downward growth, O may I, with a grey head, turn a child's heart to that figure yet, and a child's trustfulness and confidence!

Now, the tree is decorated with bright merriment, and song, and dance, and cheerfulness. And they are welcome. Innocent and welcome be they ever held, beneath the branches of the Christmas Tree, which cast no gloomy shadow! But, as it sinks into the ground, I hear a whisper going through the leaves. "This, in commemoration of the law of love and kindness, mercy and compassion. This, in remembrance of Me!"

WILLA CATHER

December Night

FATHER VAILLANT had been absent in Arizona since midsummer, and it was now December. Bishop Latour had been going through one of those periods of coldness and doubt which, from his boyhood, had occasionally settled down upon his spirit and made him feel an alien, wherever he was. He attended to his correspondence, went on his rounds among the parish priests, held services at missions that were without pastors, superintended the building of the

Much of Willa Cather's writing was devoted to the midwestern pioneer life and its heroic struggles. Cather, who grew up in Nebraska, authored several gritty midwestern novels, such as O Pioneers! and The Song of the Lark. "December Night" is from her 1927 book, Death Comes for the Archbishop.

addition to the Sisters' school: but his heart was not in
these things.

One night about three weeks before Christmas
he was lying in his bed, unable to sleep, with the sense of
failure clutching at his heart. His prayers were empty
words and brought him no refreshment. His soul had
become a barren field. He had nothing within himself to
give his priests or his people. His work seemed superfi-
cial, a house built upon the sands. His great diocese was
still a heathen country. The Indians travelled their old
road of fear and darkness, battling with evil omens and
ancient shadows. The Mexicans were children who
played with their religion.

As the night wore on, the bed on which the
Bishop lay became a bed of thorns; he could bear it no
longer. Getting up in the dark, he looked out of the window and was surprised to find that it was snowing, that
the ground was already lightly covered. The full moon,
hidden by veils of cloud, threw a pale phosphorescent
luminousness over the heavens, and the towers of the
church stood up black against this silvery fleece. Father
Latour felt a longing to go into the church to pray; but
instead he lay down again under his blankets. Then,
realizing that it was the cold of the church he shrank
from, and despising himself, he rose again, dressed
quickly, and went out into the court, throwing on over
his cassock that faithful old cloak that was the twin of
Father Vaillant's.

They had bought the cloth for those coats in

Paris, long ago, when they were young men staying at the Seminary for Foreign Missions in the rue du Bac, preparing for their first voyage to the New World. The cloth had been made up into caped riding-cloaks by a German tailor in Ohio, and lined with fox fur. Years afterward, when Father Latour was about to start on his long journey in search of his Bishopric, that same tailor had made the cloaks over and relined them with squirrel skins, as more appropriate for a mild climate. These memories and many others went through the Bishop's mind as he wrapped the trusty garment about him and crossed the court to the sacristy, with the big iron key in his hand.

The court was white with snow, and the shadows of walls and buildings stood out sharply in the faint light from the moon muffled in vapour. In the deep doorway of the sacristy he saw a crouching figure—a woman, he made out, and she was weeping bitterly. He raised her up and took her inside. As soon as he had lit a candle, he recognized her, and could have guessed her errand.

It was an old Mexican woman, called Sada, who was slave in an American family. They were Protestants, very hostile to the Roman Church, and they did not allow her to go to Mass or to receive the visits of a priest. She was carefully watched at home—but in winter, when the heated rooms of the house were desirable to the family, she was put to sleep in a woodshed. To-night, unable to sleep for the cold, she had gathered courage for this heroic action, had slipped out through the stable

door and come running up an alley-way to the House of
God to pray. Finding the front doors of the church fastened, she had made her way into the Bishop's garden
and come round to the sacristy, only to find that, too, shut
against her.

The Bishop stood holding the candle and watching her face while she spoke her few words; a dark brown
peon face, worn thin and sharp by life and sorrow. It
seemed to him that he had never seen pure goodness
shine out of a human countenance as it did from hers. He
saw that she had no stockings under her shoes—the cast-
off rawhides of her master—and beneath her frayed black
shawl was only a thin calico dress, covered with patches.
Her teeth struck together as she stood trying to control
her shivering. With one movement of his free hand the
Bishop took the furred cloak from his shoulders and put it
about her. This frightened her. She cowered under it, mur-
muring, "Ah, no, no, Padre!"

"You must obey your Padre, my daughter. Draw
that cloak about you, and we'll go into the church to
pray."

The church was utterly black except for the red
spark of the sanctuary lamp before the high altar. Taking
her hand, and holding the candle before him, he led her
across the choir to the Lady Chapel. There he began to
light the tapers before the Virgin. Old Sada fell on her
knees and kissed the floor. She kissed the feet of the Holy
Mother, the pedestal on which they stood, crying all the
while. But from the working of her face, from the beauti-

ful tremors which passed over it, he knew they were tears of ecstasy.

"Nineteen years, Father; nineteen years since I have seen the holy things of the altar!"

"All that is passed, Sada. You have remembered the holy things in your heart. We will pray together."

The Bishop knelt beside her, and they began, O *Holy Mary, Queen of Virgins.* . . .

More than once Father Vaillant had spoken to the Bishop of this aged captive. There had been much whispering among the devout women of the parish about her pitiful case. The Smiths, with whom she lived, were Georgia people, who had at one time lived in El Paso del Norte, and they had taken her back to their native State with them. Not long ago some dis- grace had come upon this family in Georgia, they had been forced to sell all their Negro slaves and flee the State. The Mexican woman they could not sell because they had no legal title to her, her position was irregular. Now that they were back in a Mexican country, the Smiths were afraid their charwoman might escape from them and find asylum among her own people, so they kept strict watch upon her. They did not allow her to go outside their own *patio*, not even to accompany her mistress to market.

Two women of the Altar Guild had been so bold as to go into the *patio* to talk with Sada when she was washing clothes, but they had been rudely driven away by the mistress of the house. Mrs. Smith had come running out into the court, half dressed, and told them that if they had business at her *casa* they were to come in by the front door, and not sneak in through the stable to frighten a poor silly creature. When they said they had come to ask Sada to go to Mass with them, she told them she had got the poor creature out of the clutches of the priests once, and would see to it that she did not fall into them again.

Even after that rebuff a very pious neighbor woman had tried to say a word to Sada through the alley door of the stable, where she was unloading wood off the burro. But the old servant had put her finger to her lips and motioned the visitor away, glancing back over her shoulder the while with such an expression of terror that the intruder hastened off, surmising that Sada would be harshly used if she were caught speaking to anyone. The good woman went immediately to Father Vaillant with this story, and he had consulted the Bishop, declaring that something ought to be done to secure the consolations of religion for the bond-woman. But the Bishop replied that the time was not yet; for the present it was inexpedient to antagonize these people. The Smiths were the leaders of a small group of low-caste Protestants who took every occasion to make trouble for the Catholics. They hung about the door of the church on festival days with mockery and loud laughter, spoke insolently to the nuns in the street, stood jeering and blaspheming when the procession went by on Corpus Christi Sunday. There were five sons in the Smith family, fellows of low habits and evil tongues. Even the two younger boys, still children, showed a vicious disposition. Tranquilino had repeatedly driven these two boys out of the Bishop's garden, where they came with their lewd companions to rob the young pear trees or to speak filth against the priests.

When they rose from their knees, Father Latour told Sada he was glad to know that she remembered her prayers so well.

"Ah, Padre, every night I say my Rosary to my Holy Mother, no matter where I sleep!" declared the old creature passionately, looking up into his face and pressing her knotted hands against her breast.

When he asked if she had her beads with her, she was confused. She kept them tied with a cord around her waist, under her clothes, as the only place she could hide them safely.

He spoke soothingly to her. "Remember this, Sada; in the year to come, and during the Novena before Christmas, I will not forget to pray for you whenever I offer the Blessed Sacrifice of the Mass. Be at rest in your heart, for I will remember you in my silent supplications before the altar as I do my own sisters and my nieces."

Never, as he afterward told Father Vaillant, had it been permitted him to behold such deep experience of the holy joy of religion as on that pale December night. He was able to feel, kneeling beside her, the preciousness of the things of the altar to her who was without possessions; the tapers, the image of the Virgin, the figures of the saints, the Cross that took away indignity from suffering and made pain and poverty a means of fellowship with Christ. Kneeling beside the much enduring bond-woman, he experienced those holy mysteries as he had done in his young manhood. He seemed able to feel all it meant to her to know that there was a Kind Woman in Heaven, though there were such cruel ones on earth. Old people, who had felt blows and toil and known the world's hard hand, need, even more than children do, a woman's tenderness. Only a Woman, divine, could know all that a woman can suffer.

Not often, indeed, had Jean Marie Latour come so near to the Fountain of all Pity as in the Lady Chapel that night; the pity that no man born of woman could ever utterly cut himself off from; that was for the murderer on the scaffold, as it was for the dying soldier or the martyr on the rack. The beautiful concept of Mary pierced the priest's heart like a sword.

"*O Sacred Heart of Mary!*" she murmured by his side, and he felt how that name was food and raiment, friend and mother to her. He received the miracle in her heart into his own, saw through her eyes, knew that his poverty was as bleak as hers. When the Kingdom of Heaven had first come into the world, into a cruel world of torture and slaves and masters, He who brought it had said, "*And whosoever is least among you, the same shall be first in the Kingdom of Heaven.*" This church was Sada's house, and he was a servant in it.

The Bishop heard the old woman's confession. He blessed her and put both hands upon her head. When he took her down the nave to let her out of the church, Sada made to lift his cloak from her shoulders. He restrained her, telling her she must keep it for her own, and sleep in it at night. But she slipped out of it hurriedly; such a thought seemed to terrify her. "No, no, Father. If they were to find it on me!" More than that, she did not accuse her oppressors. But as she put it off, she stroked the old garment and patted it as if it were a living thing that had been kind to her.

Happily Father Latour bethought him of a little silver medal, with a figure of the Virgin, he had in his pocket. He gave it to her, telling her that it had been blessed by the Holy Father himself. Now she would have a treasure to hide and guard, to adore while her watchers slept. Ah, he thought, for one who cannot read—or think—the Image, the physical form of Love!

He fitted the great key into its lock, the door swung slowly back on its wooden hinges. The peace without seemed all one with the peace in his own soul. The snow had stopped, the gauzy clouds that had ribbed the arch of heaven were now all sunk into one soft white fog bank over the Sangre de Cristo Mountains. The full moon shone high in the blue vault, majestic, lonely, benign. The Bishop stood in the doorway of his church, lost in thought, looking at the line of black footprints his departing visitor had left in the wet scurf of snow.

A 1594 BOOK OF COOKERIE

To Make a Dish of Snow

Take a pottle of sweet thick Cream, and the white of eyght Egs, and beate them altogether, with a spoone, then put them into your cream with a dishfull of Rosewater, and a dishfull of Sugar withall, then take a sticke and make it clene, and then cut it in the end foursquare, and therewith beat all the aforesaid things together, and ever as it ariseth take it off, and put it in to a Cullender, this doone, take a platter and sette an Apple in the midst of it, stick a thicke bush of Rosemary in the Apple. Then cast your Snow upon the Rosemary and fill your platter therewith, and if you have wafers cast some withall, and so serve them forthe.

"To Make a Dish of Snow" is from a 1594 English cookbook. The author is unknown.

ALEX HALEY

A Different Kind of Christmas

URING THE
Christmas Eve lunchtime, Melissa Anne Aaron hotly
challenged her father's decision not to attend the church
nativity pageant in order to go on volunteer duty with
the patrollers. Her arguing escalated until finally she
shouted, "Father, you've no right to call yourself a
Christian!"

---

*In 1988, Alex Haley wrote an unusual Christmas story—a
narrative of a slave's experience of the Christmas season. The
narrow volume* A Different Kind of Christmas *was the strik-
ing result. Haley is also the author of* The Autobiography of
Malcolm X *and* Roots, *a study of his African ancestry, for
which he won the Pulitzer Prize in 1977.*

Mr. Aaron glared at her angrily. "Don't you go too far!"

Mrs. Aaron tended to support their daughter. "Dear, she's right—once a year isn't too much to go to church."

Outnumbered and harassed, Mr. Aaron blew up.

"I'd hoped you wouldn't push me too far!" he barked at his daughter. "But since you do, I'm your father, and I'm outright forbidding your marrying this parson! I'm as much as any man for religion, but I won't permit my only daughter's hardheadedness to keep her from someone able to give her a decent life."

"All right, but if I can't marry who I want to, I'll pledge my soul I'll sure never marry who *you* want!"

"One day you'll wish you had!"

"If I can't marry him"—Melissa Anne was furious—"at least I can help him tonight!"

In her fury, she bangled on the dining-table bell. The maid appeared, nervous, knowing the hotheaded Melissa Anne. "Go bring that black harmonica player up onto the porch!" Melissa Anne commanded.

When Harpin' John arrived, Melissa Anne snapped, "Go hitch up the buggy. I want you to drive me to the church!"

As Harpin' John stood aghast, she added, "I want you to stay for the afternoon rehearsal and pull the curtain between the acts as we rehearse."

Harpin' John protested. "But ma'am, I'm the only one know when to take off my barbecue when it just

right done an' ready. I mean, ma'am, I just got to be there!"
He needed that afternoon desperately, not only to set up
the barbecue, but to oversee final details of the escape, to
reduce the chances of anything going wrong.

Melissa Anne had been spoiling for a tantrum.

She shrieked, "You heard me! You're a hired darky!
You do as I say!" She whirled. "Father!"

A dismayed Harpin' John read Mr. Aaron's
expression which conveyed that they were both caught
between a rock and a hard place.

So Harpin' John went to hitch up the buggy, his
mind racing for some answer as to how he could get
away ... for there was no way he could ignore the commands of the irate white female Melissa Anne.

THE NATIVITY pageant had been in progress
for almost an hour. A mile and a half away,
Fletcher Randall and the planter Tom Graves
were patrolling a beat around the Randall mansion
veranda, smelling the combined aromas of the pots and
tubfuls of the barbecued pork, beef, veal, and chicken
which were being kept in readiness along with the
accompaniments of cole slaw and potato salads and
dozens of sweet-potato pies, plus a liberal store of liquors
and beer that would guarantee an evening never to forget.

Fletcher had convinced his mother and father
that he should not attend the nativity pageant in order to
remain at the mansion in case some guests also might
have missed the pageant and would arrive for the

Christmas Eve barbecue early. And Tom Graves had joined Fletcher just to ensure that all was going well until his valued slave Harpin' John would be able to return from playing his harmonica for Melissa Anne Aaron at the church pageant.

Two horsemen came pounding up out of the night toward the mansion, and they headed directly for the clustering of lights about the veranda. The lean, slit-eyed chief patrolman Ned Smithers swung down off his horse and came striding directly to meet the advancing Fletcher.

"Bad news, Mr. Randall. It's not what you want to hear on Christmas Eve, but there appears to be a mass escape of slaves in the making. Three are reported missing from the Aaron plantation, and it seems that six are gone from your cabins—a patrolman's checking the premises now, and trying to find out from the rest of the darkies what happened."

Fletcher could imagine the means used to extract information. He asked, "Are you absolutely certain about this?" He hoped his dismay appeared genuine.

"About as sure as I can be, yessir. I hate to make a mess out of the senator's and your big barbecue affair here, and all—" Fletcher thought that he detected a trace of sarcasm. "But the whole thing seems to have been planned to a fare-thee-well. No telling how long they've been gone." Chief patrolman Smithers paused. "And one more thing, we're looking for Mr. Tom Graves. His wife said we'd probably find him here."

Fletcher heard Tom Graves call from behind him, "Here I am. What's the problem?"

Chief patrolman Smithers turned and nodded to his assistant, who had been standing beside his horse and now came forward, holding a bundle at his side.

Smith took the bundle, which turned out to be a brown suit-coat. He held it up to Tom Graves. "Sir, can you identify this coat?"

"Of course I can," said Tom Graves. "You see my name inked inside the collar. About a year ago I gave it to my slave, the one called Harpin' John."

Fletcher felt a sinking sensation inside his stomach.

"Where is he right now?" Smithers's tone had grown harder.

"You're asking about my slave, my property," said Tom Graves, "so I'm asking why do you want to know?"

"Well, I'll tell you. This coat was found by the patrolman who discovered the slaves were missing. It'd been left behind in one of their cabins. Question is, what was it doing there?"

"Just because you came across that damned coat doesn't mean Harpin' John had anything to do with the escape." Tom Graves was appalled at the prospect of losing a very valuable piece of property, and in truth he would also miss someone as useful and amusing as Harpin' John.

"Maybe not," Smithers said. "But I have to get hold of your slave man and ask him some hard questions, and I think we'll get some truth out of him before we finish. Where can we find him?"

"He's at the church nativity pageant," Fletcher thrust himself into the conversation. "I'll accompany you there. I think it would be best if I went in and brought him out. No need to cause a commotion in church. There'll be the devil to pay soon enough tonight. Once Harpin' John is in your hands, I'll go back and break the news to my father and all the rest."

The four men rode like the wind, and when they arrived at the church Fletcher dismounted first. "I'll be out as quickly as I can," he said, and went inside.

The nativity pageant had reached the point where the Three Wise Men, with young Parson Brown as their leader, were taking their leave of the manger where the Christ Child lay sleeping. Melissa Anne at the harpsichord was leading the background music with Harpin' John and two black slave fiddlers playing behind the performers, while the packed audience representing the planter families of the community murmured appreciatively.

When Fletcher Randall suddenly appeared in the church doorway, the reaction of Parson Brown and his companion Wise Men and Melissa Anne caused the audience to turn their heads. As Fletcher made his way briskly up the church aisle toward the stage, people stared incredulously. Fletcher passed by the front pews, in one of which sat Senator and Mrs. Randall. Their faces were disbelieving as their son stepped up onto the slightly raised stage, past Melissa Anne at her harpsichord, and went straight to black Harpin' John, who stood staring back at him, the harmonica still at his mouth.

"Follow me, *now!*" Fletcher said tautly, and turning abruptly he went double-timing to the door of the pastor's study at the church's right rear, with Harpin' John one step behind him. Once inside the small room, Fletcher said quickly, "Your horse out back?"

"Yeah, what's happened?"

"No time to talk—" He snatched open the door to the steps outside. They could hear the first rumblings of the church audience. Fletcher barked, "Get your horse, I'll grab somebody else's."

Harpin' John grunted assent, asking no questions. People were starting to emerge from the church and he could hear chief patrolman Smithers shouting as the two horses pounded away into the darkness.

"Let's split up! Go to the place I showed you, I be there!" Harpin' John shouted to Fletcher, pulling his horse toward the right and lying low against its neck to avoid the dangerous low limbs of trees he raced past.

W ITHIN THE forest, Fletcher's horse stepped into a groundhog's hole, and Fletcher tumbled off as the horse pitched forward, breaking its foreleg and screaming in pain. Fletcher struggled to his feet and then fell onto one knee. His ankle was badly hurt . . . he had never felt more alone.

But then, his chest heaving, he heard the distant

hoot-owl sound.

Fletcher put his hands up to his mouth, and tried his best to do what he had been taught.

The hoot-owl call in response was closer.

HARPIN' JOHN checked Fletcher's ankle. "Well, we lucky, it ain't broke. But the way it already swellin', look like a real bad sprain." He looked directly into Fletcher's face. "Wasn't sure I'd ever see you no more."

Fletcher said, "I thought you were a goner, too—"

"Would have been, hadn't been for you." Harpin' John took a long pause. "You didn't have to do what you done. How come you come in after me?"

Fletcher thought about that. "Tell you the truth, I never thought about it. I just did, that's all."

"Well, we can't rest here no longer, we got to git movin'. I know they after us, probably with dogs by now, an' we got to be either long gone or hid mighty good by daylight." Again he appraised Fletcher. "You a big man, but I can carry you to the horse, and us can both ride to a better hiding place."

Fletcher pushed himself upright again, fending away Harpin' John's help, to test himself. He tried the ankle. He winced with the pain. He managed about three hopping steps and stopped.

"It hurts. But I can make steps, especially if I lean on your shoulder. But I'd best wait just a minute—it really hurts."

"Did they all get away?" Harpin' John asked.

"I think. It sounded like it, what little I heard."

"Well, can you tell me what happened, I mean what went wrong?"

"I sure can. You gave somebody a coat, and he left it hanging in his cabin. The patrollers found it with Tom Graves's name inside, and he told them he gave it to you."

"I be damn! You mean 'ceptin' for that, we wouldn't be out here now? All we did, and that one little thing went wrong! If I could've got out'n that pageant, I really b'lieve I'd of noticed old Uncle Ben didn't wear my coat. I should've kept it when he told me he thought it was too pretty for him to wear, anyway."

Harpin' John looked at Fletcher Randall. "Well, for sure, neither one of us can't never go back. What you goin' to do? You figured out yet where you goin'?"

"I haven't had time for that. I wasn't planning on this."

Harpin' John reflected for a moment. "You know, lotsa people don't realize how many white folks risks all you got, even your lives, because you don't believe slavery's right."

Fletcher thought a little while. Then he asked, "What about you? Where are you going?"

"Jes' up North, that's all I know for now." Harpin' John chuckled. "Maybe I can start me a little business cookin' good barbecue—I can do that, an' make a little music."

Fletcher determinedly pushed himself up again.

He gestured that he was ready to try walking, with Harpin' John's assistance. Two hours later, deeper in the forest, they crossed a wide stream, and were confident they had eluded their pursuers.

Suddenly Harpin' John plucked from his pocket his harmonica, which he cupped against his mouth, and brought forth his patented resounding railroad locomotive *chuffing* sound.

Abruptly he stopped, whacking the harmonica against one knee. "Hey, lemme quit actin' a fool, 'cause you know what?" He stared up at the radiant North Star, joined by Fletcher. "'Cause this here is Christmas morning now—won't be but a couple of hours 'fore the day breaks."

Again he raised the harmonica, saying to Fletcher, "Now here's a tune I don't know what it is, I jes' sort of remember it from hearin' it bein' played an' sung last Christmas when I was ridin' my horse amongst where some them new German emigrant peoples moved in the other end of Ashe County. I can't remember but jes' two sounds of the German words they was singin, they sounded something like '*Stille Nacht* ...'"

Harpin' John cupped his harmonica. "But I know the tune they played went like this."

He played. Fletcher heard the melody of "Silent Night" as the Christmas moonlight bathed the faces of the black man playing and the white man listening.

When Harpin' John finished, neither man said a word. Then the pair of them resumed walking, silhouetted against the Christmas early morning sky.

Fletcher realized that now his life had changed forever, too. He thought about his parents with a sense of pain and loss that he knew both they and he would be a long time absorbing and coming to terms with. He had made an irrevocable break with his past. He knew he had made a wreck of their lives. His father's political career would become a shambles, and in Senator Randall's eyes, indeed all Southerners' eyes, Fletcher Randall would forever be a traitor. As for his mother, she'd be devastated, and he wondered agonizingly whether she would ever recover from the shame he'd brought upon her, and from the ache of losing her only child. It would be, to both of them, as if he were dead. But whatever the ache of the present and uncertainties of his future, he knew now that by not living for himself, he was learning to live with himself, at last. He'd told Harpin' John that he wasn't sure where he'd go, or what he'd do. But he remembered one thing for sure: he had some friends in Philadelphia.

W . H . A U D E N

The Meditation of Simeon

IMEON

As long as the apple had not been entirely digested, as long as there remained the least understanding between Adam and the stars, rivers and horses with whom he had once known complete intimacy, as long as Eve could share in any way with the moods of the rose or the ambitions of the swallow, there was still a hope that the effects

---

W.H. Auden wrote his best-known poems in the 1930s as a politically active leftist. Later in life, Auden's sympathies veered toward Christianity, as evidenced in pieces like "The Meditation of Simeon." His conviction became so strong that he even published revised, more conservative versions of his early work. Auden's books The Orators, Collected Poems *and* On This Island *are considered pillars of modern poetry.*

of the poison would wear off, that the exile from Paradise was only a bad dream, that the Fall had not occurred in fact.

CHORUS
When we woke, it was day; we went on weeping.

SIMEON
As long as there were any roads to amnesia and anaesthesia still to be explored, any rare wine or curiosity of cuisine as yet untested, any erotic variation as yet unimagined or unrealised, any method of torture as yet undevised, any style of conspicuous waste as yet unindulged, any eccentricity of mania or disease as yet unrepresented, there was still a hope that man has not been poisoned but transformed, that Paradise was not an eternal state from which he had been forever expelled, but a childish state which he had permanently outgrown, that the Fall had occurred by necessity.

CHORUS
We danced in the dark, but were not deceived.

SIMEON
As long as there were any experiments still to be undertaken in restoring that order in which desire had once rejoiced to be reflected, any code of equity and obligation upon which some society had not yet been founded, any species of property of which the value had not yet

been appreciated, any talent that had not yet won private devotion and public honour, any rational concept of the Good or intuitive feeling for the Holy that had not yet found its precise and beautiful expression, any technique of contemplation or ritual of sacrifice and praise that had not yet been properly conducted, any faculty of mind or body that had not yet been thoroughly disciplined, there was still a hope that some antidote might be found, that the gates of Paradise had indeed slammed to, but with the exercise of a little patience and ingenuity would be unlocked, that the Fall had occurred by accident.

CHORUS
Lions came loping into the lighted city.

SIMEON
Before the Positive could manifest Itself specifically, it was necessary that nothing should be left that negation could remove; the emancipation of Time from Space had first to be complete, the Revolution of the Images, in which the memories rose up and cast into subjection the senses by Whom hitherto they had been enslaved, successful beyond their wildest dreams, the mirror in which the Soul expected to admire herself so perfectly polished that her natural consolation of vagueness should be utterly withdrawn.

CHORUS
We looked at our Shadow, and, Lo, it was lame.

SIMEON

Before the Infinite could manifest Itself in the finite, it was necessary that man should first have reached that point along his road to Knowledge where, just as it rises from the swamps of Confusion onto the sunny slopes of Objectivity, it forks in opposite directions toward the One and the Many; where, therefore, in order to proceed at all, he must decide which is Real and which only Appearance, yet at the same time cannot escape the knowledge that his choice is arbitrary and subjective.

CHORUS

Promising to meet, we parted forever.

SIMEON

Before the Unconditional could manifest Itself under the conditions of existence, it was necessary that man should first have reached the ultimate frontier of consciousness, the secular limit of memory beyond which there remained but one thing for him to know, his Original Sin, but of this it is impossible for him to become conscious because it is itself what conditions his will to knowledge. For as long as he was in Paradise he could not sin by any conscious intention or act: his as yet unfallen will could only rebel against the truth by taking flight into an unconscious lie; he could only eat of the Tree of the Knowledge of Good and Evil by forgetting that its existence was a fiction of the Evil One, that there is only the Tree of Life.

CHORUS

The bravest drew back on the brink of the Abyss.

SIMEON

From the beginning until now God spoke through His prophets. The Word aroused the uncomprehending depths of their flesh to a witnessing fury, and their witness was this: that the Word should be made Flesh. Yet their witness could only be received as long as it was vaguely misunderstood, as long as it seemed either to be neither impossible nor necessary, or necessary but not impossible, or impossible but not necessary; and the prophecy could not therefore be fulfilled. For it could only be fulfilled when it was no longer possible to receive, because it was clearly understood as absurd. The Word could not be made Flesh until men had reached a state of absolute contradiction between clarity and despair in which they would have no choice but either to accept absolutely or to reject absolutely, yet in their choice there should be no element of luck, for they would be fully conscious of what they were accepting or rejecting.

CHORUS

The eternal spaces were congested and depraved.

SIMEON

But here and now the Word which is implicit in the Beginning and in the End is become immediately explicit, and that which hitherto we could only passively fear as the incomprehensible I AM, henceforth we may actively love with comprehension that THOU ART. Wherefore, having seen Him, not in some prophetic vision of what might be, but with the eyes of our own weakness as to what actually is, we are bold to say that we have seen our salvation.

CHORUS
Now and forever, we are not alone.

SIMEON
By the event of this birth the true significance of all other events is defined, for of every other occasion it can be said that it could have been different, but of this birth it is the case that it could in no way be other than it is. And by the existence of this Child, the proper value of all other existences is given, for of every other creature it can be said that it has extrinsic importance but of this Child it is the case that He is in no sense a symbol.

CHORUS
We have right to believe that we really exist.

SIMEON
By Him is dispelled the darkness wherein the fallen will cannot distinguish between temptation and sin, for in Him we become fully conscious of Necessity as our free-

dom to be tempted, and of Freedom as our necessity to have faith. And by Him is illuminated the time in which we execute those choices through which our freedom is realised or prevented, for the course of History is predictable in the degree to which all men love themselves, and spontaneous in the degree to which each man loves God and through Him his neighbour.

CHORUS
The distresses of choice are our chance to be blessed.

SIMEON
Because in Him the Flesh is united to the Word without magical transformation, Imagination is redeemed from promiscuous fornication with her own images. The tragic conflict of Virtue with Necessity is no longer confined to the Exceptional Hero; for disaster is not the impact of a curse upon a few great families, but issues continually from the hubris of every tainted will. Every invalid is Roland defending the narrow pass against hopeless odds, every stenographer Brunnhilde refusing to renounce her lover's ring which came into existence through the renunciation of love.

Nor is the Ridiculous a species any longer of the Ugly; for since of themselves all men are without merit, all are ironically assisted to their comic bewilderment by the Grace of God. Every Cabinet Minister is the wood-cutter's simple-minded son to whom the fishes and the crows are always whispering the whereabouts of the

Dancing Water or the Singing Branch, every heiress the washerwoman's butterfingered daughter on whose pillow the fairy keeps laying the herb that could cure the Prince's mysterious illness.

Nor is there any situation which is essentially more or less interesting than another. Every tea-table is a battlefield littered with old catastrophes and haunted by the vague ghosts of vast issues, every martyrdom an occasion for flip cracks and sententious oratory.

Because in Him all passions find a logical In-Order-That, by Him is the perpetual recurrence of Art assured.

CHORUS
Safe in His silence, our songs are at play.

SIMEON
Because in Him the Word is united to the Flesh without loss of perfection, Reason is redeemed from incestuous fixation on her own Logic, for the One and the Many are simultaneously revealed as real. So that we may no longer, with the Barbarians, deny the Unity, asserting that there are as many gods as there are creatures, nor, with the philosophers, deny the Multiplicity, asserting that God is One who has no need of friends and is indifferent to a World of Time and Quantity and Horror which He did not create, nor, with Israel, may we limit the co-inherence of the One and Many to a special case, asserting that God is only concerned with and of concern to that People whom

out of all that He created He has chosen for His own.

For the Truth is indeed One, without which is no salvation, but the possibilities of real knowledge are as many as are the creatures in the very real and most exciting universe that God creates with and for His love, and it is not Nature which is one public illusion, but we who have each our many private illusions about Nature.

Because in Him abstraction finds a passionate For-The-Sake-Of, by Him is the continuous development of Science assured.

CHORUS
Our lost Appearances are saved by His love.

SIMEON
And because of His visitation, we may no longer desire God as if He were lacking: our redemption is no longer a question of pursuit but of surrender to Him who is always and everywhere present. Therefore at every moment we pray that, following Him, we may depart from our anxiety into His peace.

CHORUS
Its errors forgiven, may our Vision come home.

E . E .   C U M M I N G S

little tree

ITTLE TREE
little silent Christmas tree
you are so little
you are more like a flower

who found you in the green forest
and were you very sorry to come away?

---

*American poet and novelist e.e. cummings is responsible for
some of the great oddball poetry of the 20th century. His
hallmarks—eccentric typography and insistence on all lower
case characters—are immediately recognizable. cummings
also penned a highly acclaimed autobiographical novel,* The
Enormous Room. *"little tree" is from his 1923 collection*
Tulips and Chimneys.

see   i will comfort you
because you smell so sweetly

i will kiss your cool bark
and hug you safe and tight
just as your mother would,
only don't be afraid

look   the spangles
that sleep all the year in a dark box
dreaming of being taken out and allowed to
            shine,
the balls the chains red and gold the fluffy
            threads,

put up your little arms
and i'll give them all to you to hold
every finger shall have its ring
and there won't be a single place dark or
            unhappy

then when you're quite dressed
you'll stand in the window for everyone to see
and how they'll stare!
oh but you'll be very proud

and my little sister and i will take hands

＊

and looking up at our beautiful tree
we'll dance and sing
"Noel Noel"

Credits